"Is it unlocked?" Lauren glanced toward his truck.

In response Bren moved to the passenger side and opened it. She hadn't had a man open the door for her in...well, a long, long time.

"Thanks."

He nodded. She had to look away.

Great. Less than two minutes in his company and it was all she could do to look him in the eye. He caused her heart to pump at what felt like a million beats per minute.

"Need help up?" he asked, holding out a supporting hand.

"No, no."

But he helped her anyway, his hand capturing her elbow and gently guiding her. She might have moved, but inside everything froze, her breathing, her heart, even her vision as she stared straight ahead. And then he let her go and she wilted into the cab of his truck, the door sealing with a pop.

Oh, dear Lord.

How would she ever make it through the next few hours?

Dear Reader,

I've spent a lot of time at junior rodeos, but not because I have a kid who likes to compete. Actually, I have a kid who's a junior rodeo queen—complete with the big silver crown.

Recently, as I watched my daughter proudly represent her rodeo, I spotted an anxious mom helping her steer-riding son, and I was grateful I didn't have to deal with that. I couldn't imagine watching my kid compete in such a dangerous sport. I found myself wondering if the woman was a single mom, and if so, how she managed on her own.

I love it when an idea for a book comes to me full-blown. Authors will tell you the "what if" game is how stories are born. I started thinking about that single mom, imagining that her life had been torn to shreds, yet she'd made it through to the other side. That poor woman at that rodeo has no idea she was the inspiration for a romance novel.

Lauren Danners is my favorite kind of character. Smart. Driven. A great mom. She's pulled herself up by her bootstraps and changed her life all on her own. She doesn't need tough-guy lawman Bren Connelly. She's doing just fine. Or is she?

You'll have to read the book to find out. As always, I hope you enjoy my grown-up-girl horse story. I always try to write about ranching and the animals I love. I hope you like reading about them. Drop me a line if you're so inclined. I'm on Facebook at Facebook.com/pamelabritton.

Pam

HER COWBOY LAWMAN

—

PAMELA BRITTON

⬦ HARLEQUIN® WESTERN ROMANCE

Recycling programs
for this product may
not exist in your area.

ISBN-13: 978-0-373-75746-6

Her Cowboy Lawman

Copyright © 2017 by Pamela Britton

Printed in U.S.A.

HARLEQUIN®
www.Harlequin.com

With more than a million books in print, **Pamela Britton** likes to call herself the best-known author nobody's ever heard of. Of course, that changed thanks to a certain licensing agreement with that little racing organization known as NASCAR.

But before the glitz and glamour of NASCAR, Pamela wrote books that were frequently voted the best of the best by the *Detroit Free Press*, Barnes & Noble (two years in a row) and *RT Book Reviews*. She's won numerous awards, including a National Readers' Choice Award and a nomination for the Romance Writers of America Golden Heart® Award.

When not writing books, Pamela is a reporter for a local newspaper. She's also a columnist for the *American Quarter Horse Journal*.

Books by Pamela Britton

Harlequin Western Romance

Cowboys in Uniform

Her Rodeo Hero
His Rodeo Sweetheart
The Ranger's Rodeo Rebel

Harlequin American Romance

Rancher and Protector
The Rancher's Bride
A Cowboy's Pride
A Cowboy's Christmas Wedding
A Cowboy's Angel
The Texan's Twins
Kissed by a Cowboy

Visit the Author Profile page
at Harlequin.com for more titles.

Dedicated with heartfelt gratitude to all the men and women who protect this country.

Chapter One

Lauren Danners leaned against one of the five wooden columns that supported the rodeo's announcer's stand and tried not to hyperventilate. In front of her—a mere two feet away—a young steer tried to jump out of a rodeo chute. A flurry of voices called, "Watch out, watch out," around her, but she didn't look away. She had eyes only for the young boy intending to sit atop the steer—her ten-year-old son.

Please, God. Don't let him get hurt.

"You know you could always watch from the grandstands," said a man wearing a black cowboy hat and a commiserating smile. "You could put your head between your legs up there if you feel like you're gonna vomit."

She pulled herself out from beneath a haze of panic to note the man had a gold star pinned to the front of his polo shirt, one with the word Sheriff clearly etched into the metal.

"Bren," someone said, another cowboy, this one older and with a bushy gray mustache that matched the hair beneath his ratty old cowboy hat. "I would have thought for sure you'd be helping out." He nodded toward the bucking chutes.

"Nah. They've got things under control."

The man beside her sounded like a cartoon character of a Texas lawman. Low drawl. Deep voice. Slow words. But they were in Via Del Caballo, California. A long ways away from Texas.

"You new around here?" asked Bren.

She could barely see Kyle between the half dozen men helping him mount his first rodeo steer. Her son hadn't looked once in her direction. Not once. She didn't know whether to be offended or relieved because clearly he'd decided to focus on the task at hand. That was good, because if he'd glanced at her with fear on his face and terror in his eyes, she would have run over to him and ripped him off the dang cow...or steer...or whatever it was called.

"Just moved here," she admitted, recognizing the words for what they were. A lifeline. A way to distract her from the fact that her son was about to do something she really didn't want him to do but that his uncle thought would be "good for him." And now her brother was the one up in the grandstands watching from a distance while she was the one about to throw up.

"He'll be okay," said the man next to her. "The steers aren't half as bad as bulls. That's why they use them for the junior rodeos. The most they'll do is buck a few times and maybe run off."

She felt the blood drain from her face. *Run off.* With her son strapped to his back. Good Lord, she didn't need that visual.

"Look, Officer..."

"*Sheriff* Connelly," he said, holding out his hand. "Brennan Connelly."

"Lauren Danners." She took the hand, and she wasn't

so preoccupied that she didn't notice how firm his grip was. And that his tan arms had tight cords of muscle running along the length of them, and that dark hair spotted the surface, the ends bleached blond from the sun. Good-looking didn't even begin to describe him.

"Nice to meet you, Miss Danners." He tipped his hat, something she'd only ever seen men do in movies.

"Same here." She smiled as brightly as she could. "But please don't take this wrong. I appreciate your friendliness, I really do, but talking means I have to open my mouth and I really am afraid I might spontaneously vomit all over the front of you and that would only add insult to injury where this day is concerned."

His smile grew. A couple feet away, the steer Kyle tried to mount had settled down and the sudden quiet made her stomach turn even more. She'd been hoping they'd let the steer go. That he'd get to try riding another one, a calmer one. Maybe one that was so old it could barely get out of the gate. Obviously not. She stood on a raised wooden dais, one that allowed spectators to peer down into the rodeo chutes, and against her better judgment she took a few steps forward, bringing her so close she could smell the steer and the sweat of the men around her.

"Easy there, Sparky." Bren placed a hand on her shoulder. She barely noticed. The rodeo announcer told everyone to put their hands together because a local kid new to riding steers was about to make his debut, which meant...

The gate opened.

Kyle.

Her son, her baby boy, shot through the air. He didn't ride for one second, much less eight, arms akimbo, limbs splayed as he landed on his backside. She knew this because she'd jammed herself up against the edge of the chute without even realizing it, her son in a heap practically at her feet. Then and only then did he look around for her, his eyes catching her own, the grin beneath the metal face guard attached to his helmet unmistakable.

"That was *great*!"

She turned around and the man behind her caught her. She struggled for a moment because she really did think she would be sick, but he wouldn't let her go.

"Don't ruin this for him," he said softly. "Just breathe. The sickness will go away. He's all right."

She clung to him even though she'd just met him, even though a part of her felt outrage that he wouldn't let her go, even though it took all her strength to do as he asked and breathe.

"Look. He's getting up."

She turned. Sure enough, Kyle slowly stood, his beige protective vest, his green shirt and his jeans all covered in mud. In the arena, the steer had already left through the exit gate. Her son waved to the crowd, who applauded in response, and she could swear she heard her brother yell, "Attaboy, Kyle!" all the way from the grandstands.

"I don't think I can do this again," she muttered.

She made sure that Kyle really was okay before turning back to the man who stared down at her. She had to have been distracted earlier because this time it hit her. The size of him. The breadth of him. The gorgeous golden-brown color of his eyes. Those eyes gave her such an odd sense of déjà vu that she took a step back, almost falling over the top of the chute.

"Whoa." His hands caught her shoulders. "Careful there."

"Sorry." She forced herself to smile. "I'm a little light-headed."

Because you almost tossed your cookies.

Nope. Not because of that. She was long past the age of swooning over handsome men, but that didn't mean she couldn't acknowledge when one took her breath away. This one did. And he seemed so familiar somehow. As if she'd known him all her life. She'd had the same sensation when Kyle had been born and she'd stared into his eyes for the first time.

"Mom! Are you proud of me?"

It was as if fate had turned on the stereo of her inner musings and called up the voice of her son. Kyle had crawled back over the chute, cowbell clanging, bull rope dangling, a grin she'd seen only on Christmas morning plastered across his face.

"I stayed on for at least a minute."

She almost laughed. She was too aware of the man standing next to her. Kyle suddenly became aware of him, too, drawing himself up. She'd seen that reaction before. She rarely brought men home, but when she did, it was as if Kyle bristled invisible hair.

"You did great," Sheriff Connelly said, tapping the top of her son's helmet.

Kyle jerked the plastic cap off his head, hazel eyes never wavering from Sheriff Connelly. The crowd of men who'd helped had since moved on. They bustled around the next rider as the announcer droned on about something she couldn't quite catch. Her son's hair stuck straight up, but instead of the scowl she expected to see, all she spotted was something close to stunned surprise.

"You're Brennan Connelly."

Whoa. Wait. *What?* She knew the name. Her big brother had told her all about the man who'd walked away from the sport of rodeo to join the military. The world champion turned lawman.

"I am," he said with an easy smile.

"Your poster is hanging on my wall."

That's why he looked so familiar. That's why she'd been taken aback by the eerie sensation that she'd met him before. She *had* met him before. In her son's bedroom. Every night she saw this man's face when she kissed her son good-night, a much younger version, more lean, less…friendly looking, but still devastatingly handsome. If she were honest, she'd gone back to her own bedroom and…

No, no, no. Don't go down that road. Not now. Not with the real thing standing here in front of you.

"My poster?" Bren asked, including her in his grin. "How the heck did you find one of those?

"I ordered it online. My uncle Jax told me about you. About how you lived close by and about how you won the world championship, but that you walked away from it all right after and became a Green Beret. I looked you up, watched your ride on the internet. It was awesome."

Green Beret? No wonder the man oozed testosterone.

"These days he coaches our high school rodeo team," said the same old man who'd greeted him earlier. He patted Bren on the back. "Taken them all the way to the national finals four years in a row. Almost won the whole shebang this year. We would have, too, if Will's hand hadn't slipped out of his wrap."

"You teach kids how to ride?"

It was Kyle who'd spoken and she recognized the

tone in his voice. She knew what was coming next, moved to intercept the words. "Nice to meet you, Sheriff Connelly. Thanks for helping settle my nerves."

"You were nervous?" her son asked before turning back to Brennan. "Can you teach me?"

"Of course he can," said the gray-haired man Lauren suddenly wanted to kill. He had skin as worn as his blue jeans, but the blue eyes were still sharp as a tack. "Been teaching kids for years."

"Now, Samson," Bren said, patting his friend on the shoulder. "This nice young woman doesn't want my help."

"*I* want your help," said her son. "I really need to learn how to ride, but my mom won't let me practice because she thinks all bull riders are dumb. Actually, she thinks everything to do with the rodeo is dumb. I've been trying to tell her that isn't true, and that I could get a scholarship or something for college if I'm good enough and that I could make lots of money. *Ouch.*" Her son jerked away from her. "Mom."

She hadn't even realized she'd dug her hands into her son's shirt.

Earth, just swallow me whole.

When she spotted the amused twitch in Bren's eyes, she felt her face flame with color, too.

Dumb, huh? his grin seemed to ask.

"Kid's right," Samson interrupted with a firm nod. "There's intercollegiate teams that compete for titles. Sure, it's not as glamorous as, say, football or basketball, but it's a good, clean sport." The man all but wagged a finger at her. "You don't hear about no bull riders beating up their girlfriends or making money on fighting dogs. Rodeo's an honorable sport that's known for turning boys into men. Just look at Brennan here. Rodeo team in college. Went pro for a couple years, then went off to serve his country."

Oh, dear Lord.

"I know." She glared at Kyle, silently telling her son they'd have words later. Kyle had the grace to look slightly abashed. "But he's never ridden anything in his life. We just moved to my brother's ranch outside of town and now Kyle thinks he's a cowboy, and I told him it takes more than petting a horse to make you a cowboy. Now he's got it in his head that he can be a bull rider, and my brother encourages it all. The man all but blackmailed me into entering him today, something I didn't want to do, because I think he needs to learn how to ride a horse before he can ride a steer, and clearly I was right about that because he didn't stick on for more than a second today."

"It was longer than a second," Kyle protested.

She was rambling, feeling stupid and out of place and, yes, guilty thanks to the look of recrimination on the old man's face.

"Who's your brother?" Bren asked.

The question threw her for a moment. "Jax," she said. "Jax Stone. He owns Dark Horse Ranch."

She should have known the name would be recognized. If she knew anything about Via Del Caballo, it was that it was a small town and everyone seemed to know everybody.

"That's that newfangled therapy ranch at the old Reynolds place, isn't it?" Samson asked. "For army vets."

"Actually, it's for veterans with post-traumatic stress

disorder, and he only bought a portion of the Reynoldses' place. He didn't buy it all."

But he could have. Her brother could afford to buy pretty much whatever he wanted, like her son's new bull-riding vest and the helmet, which had been a birthday present to Kyle last month. She'd wanted to kill her brother at the time, only she'd spotted the pride and joy and excitement on her son's face, emotions she hadn't seen since before Paul had died.

"I've heard a lot of good things about Jax Stone," Bren said. "Been meaning to drive over to his place and introduce myself."

"You could do that today," Kyle said excitedly. "He's here at the rodeo."

"I'm sure Mr. Connelly has more important things to do than meet my brother," Lauren said gently, forcing a smile.

"Actually, I don't."

She should have known he'd say that.

"Mom, pleeeease?" Kyle begged. "Let's go over there right now, ask him what he thought about my ride."

The announcer's voice grew loud again and they all turned to watch as a steer burst from the chutes, its rider clinging to its back. One jump, two, three. The steer bucked left and then right, the kid never once losing his grip.

"That's Pete Hale, one of Bren's students," Samson said. "Gonna make it big if he keeps this up."

The air horn blew. The boy made it look as if he hopped off a carousel horse. Kyle's hand found her own. She glanced down, and she saw it then. The hope. The desire. The need to be good at something when he'd only ever been bad at sports. Too short for basketball. Too skinny for football. Perfect for riding steers.

Don't ruin this for him.

She'd been angry about Bren Connelly saying that, but he'd been right. If her son had seen how badly she'd been affected by his ride, he might have realized just how much she didn't want him riding. He'd give it up for her. He was that kind of kid. Always had been— even before Paul's death.

Damn it.

"All right. Let's go."

"Awesome!" Kyle cried.

Chapter Two

Nervous mothers.

They were the bane of a bull rider's life. His own mom had given up going to rodeos. He suspected Kyle Danners's mom would be no different. Once she let go of the apron strings, she'd realize it was easier to sit at home and wait for a phone call. Out of sight, out of mind. That's what his mom used to say.

"My uncle Jax will love meeting you," Kyle was saying as they walked around the edge of the rodeo arena. The Via Del Caballo Rodeo Grounds was a small venue compared to Redding's or Cheyenne's. They'd used the hillside next to the arena for grandstands, building right into the side of them, and it might be a junior rodeo, but it was still packed. Young and old sat beneath the partly cloudy skies. By the time they made their way through the horses and people milling around the outside of the arena, the steer riding was almost over.

"Pete Hale is going to win it," Kyle said, whipping around to face him.

"Looks that way."

"I can't wait for you to teach me how to ride, too."

"Kyle," Lauren interrupted. "You shouldn't assume Sheriff Connelly wants you for a student."

People watched him walk by, but it was like old home week for him. Usually he spent his time at a rodeo behind the chutes and not in uniform. Half the town seemed to call his name or wave or simply smile. It was a campaign year, which meant every handshake might count for a vote, although in truth he took pride in knowing the names and faces of many Via Del Caballo citizens.

"Besides, it looks like he probably won't have time for you."

"Actually, I might have time to help him out."

"Really?" Kyle cried so loudly a few people glanced in his direction. "Awesome!"

"Your mom's right, though. The best thing for you is to learn how to ride. And not just regular riding but how to jump."

"What?" Kyle said.

His mom looked just as perplexed, but she'd stopped at the end of an aisle and he could see a man staring at her, a man a few years younger than he was, which only solidified his earlier assumption that Lauren Danners was at least ten years his junior. Far too young for him, and made to look even younger with her tiny little nose and big hazel eyes. He'd wondered where her husband was.

"You don't mean over obstacles, do you?"

He bit back a smile. "Actually, I do."

Whatever she was about to say was interrupted by a man calling out, "Good job, little dude."

"Did you see me, Uncle Jax?" Kyle asked with pride on his face. "I did it. I didn't chicken out."

"I saw."

They had to bump and nudge their way down the

aisle. Someone called out his name again, and Bren waved at them blindly.

"Jax, this is Bren Connelly," his sister said, sitting next to her brother, the resemblance startling. They both had dark hair and hazel eyes, but Lauren's were more green than gold. Looking at them sitting there next to each other, he realized Jax was quite a few years older than his sister.

"Wait a second," Jax said. "Brennan Connelly. The bull rider?"

"One and the same."

They shook hands. "Heard a lot about you."

"Guesswhatguesswhatguesswhat?" Kyle bounced in his seat.

"What?" asked Jax.

"Sheriff Connelly is going to teach me how to ride steers."

Jax's brows lifted in surprise. "You teach steer riding?"

"Kyle, stop." Lauren shook her head, shooting both men a look of apology, her long dark hair falling loose around her shoulder. "He has a bad habit of assuming things."

"But he said he would."

"Actually, what I said was that first you need to learn how to ride."

"You said jump," Kyle said.

"Which means riding."

The rodeo announcer's voice drowned out the sound of the crowd and they all turned and watched the last rider burst from the chute. The boy threw his arm up in the air and rode for one jump, two and then three. Bren wondered if the kid would cover for eight, but the steer changed directions and the poor boy didn't stand a chance. In a heartbeat it was all over.

"Pete won!" Kyle said with youthful enthusiasm tinged by hero worship. "That's so cool."

"Actually, he hasn't officially won yet. There's more steer riding tomorrow."

People began to stand up. The rodeo announcer thanked everyone for attending. Jax Stone didn't move.

"You said he needed to learn how to jump. As in horses, yes?"

Bren nodded. "He should take some lessons from your neighbor Natalie Reynolds. She's been working with a few of my kids."

"I don't understand," Lauren said.

He turned to her, although that meant facing her again and being reminded of how young she was. "It teaches them how to center themselves on an animal's back," he explained. "Like a pendulum or a teeter-totter. The rider stays straight up and down while the horse— and later a steer or bull—rocks beneath them. Once a rider learns how to stay centered, the rest is easy."

Jax was nodding. "Makes sense."

"I don't have to wear those riding tights, do I?"

"Kyle, really." Lauren pursed her lips and shook her head. "I haven't agreed for you to take lessons with Sheriff Connelly. I'm not even sure what he charges."

"I've told you a hundred times, don't worry about money," her brother said.

"And I've told you I didn't move out here to accept your charity. It's bad enough I'm living in your house-keeper's quarters."

"I built that for you."

"Yeah, for when I visited. Not permanently."

"So what if you live there now?"

"I refuse to live with my brother."

Lauren glanced in Bren's direction, clearly embarrassed by their outburst. "Sorry," she said. "You don't need to hear our dirty laundry."

Kyle stood up. "It's not dirty laundry. It's true. Ever since Dad died, Uncle Jax has wanted us to live with him, but you wouldn't let us."

"Kyle!"

"I have eyes and ears, Mom. I see how hard you're struggling to finish school and take care of me and everything. But it doesn't have to be like that. I want to live with Uncle Jax. You're the one that's making this hard."

He turned and ran off. Lauren tried to grab his hand. She missed.

"I'll go after him," Jax said, standing, but he had an admonishing look on his face, too. "You should listen to your son, Lauren."

They both watched them leave, and Bren could tell Lauren wished she could slip through the slats in the grandstand.

"Sorry," she muttered.

"Don't apologize. I understand."

She met his gaze and her eyes asked the question *Do you?* and he found himself wondering why a pretty little thing like her had so much sadness in her eyes. He looked away from her, troubled by how easily her sorrow tugged at his heart. The grandstands were nearly empty now, just the two of them sitting there. They both watched as Jax caught up with his nephew, stopping him with a hand on his shoulder. He still wore his rodeo number and it flapped in a sudden breeze as he came to a stop. He didn't know what Jax said to his nephew, but the boy's shoulders slumped. He reached for his uncle's hand and together they walked out of the grandstands together.

"A year ago I would never have thought my brother would warm up to my son like that."

He glanced back at her, the same breeze kicking her brown hair across her face, Bren admitting once again how pretty she was. "What do you mean?"

She peeked down at her nails. "There was a time when the military was his whole life. And after that, when his business was all that mattered to him."

"Darkhorse Tactical Solutions. DTS. I know."

She smiled slightly. "Everyone knows everything about everyone in this town."

He smiled, too. "I'm the local lawman. I make it my business to know who's moved in and out."

But she'd tuned him out, he could tell. She stared after her son with such a keen sense of longing it made his heart tighten in pity all over again.

"He begged me to move here." She looked over at him. "We came here for a visit last year—before the house was finished—and it was all I could do to drag Kyle back to the Bay Area. He kept going on and on about his uncle Jax and his big ranch and how we could move to Via Del Caballo."

"So you did."

"We did, and to be honest, it's a lot easier to make ends meet when you live in a small town, and it helps that my brother's offered us free room and board." She shifted, placing her elbows on her knees, resting her head in her palms. She looked so young then. Years ago she would have been exactly his type. No fake hair.

Very little makeup. Easy smile. He'd been drawn to her the moment he'd spotted her standing there by the chutes.

"But I can't stay there forever." She straightened again. "The whole point of my going back to school was so that I could finish my degree and find a good job."

"What do you do?"

"Nursing." Her smile turned bashful. "I've always felt compelled to help others. Turns out it's a family trait."

"You could work for a local nursing home."

She shook her head. "No. I need to make enough money to support me and my kid. That's the whole point. I want a good life for him, the best. That's only going to happen at a big hospital, which is why I'm going for a bachelor of science in nursing"

"So this is just temporary?"

She let her feet slide back to the ground. "Before the year's out, I'll have graduated and found a new job, and I don't think Kyle likes the idea."

He didn't blame the kid. He hated the big cities. It was why he'd settled back down here once his military career had ended.

"So let him enjoy himself while he's around," he said. "Let him take some riding lessons and maybe get on a few more steers."

Her eyes became serious. "I've seen what happens to bull riders. I've been an intern in an ER."

"All the more reason to make sure he learns how to ride correctly. He could have been injured today coming off that close to the chutes. He needs to learn how to fall in addition to how to ride."

Her brows lifted and he could tell she understood his

point, but then she glanced toward where her son and Jax had disappeared It was almost as if he could sense the thoughts going on in her head, an inner battle of some sort. She must have arrived at a decision because she straightened suddenly, nodded, turned back to him. "So will you teach him?"

Would he?

Despite what he'd said earlier, he hadn't planned on taking Kyle on as a student. His focus was high school rodeo. But he wasn't proof against the imploring look on her face.

"I could maybe help him out a little bit."

She reached for his hand. Bren glanced down, noting how refined her hands were against his own, how they were so white and his were dark. Her skin was soft and smooth. His was worn and calloused. Old and young. Worn and new.

"Thank you."

When he looked back into her eyes, he suddenly wished he were in his twenties again. Now he'd be cradle-robbing—and he wasn't about to do that. Not now. Not ever.

"No problem."

But as they stood together, she flung her hair over her shoulder and the wind caught it and blew it around her face, and he realized she could be a serious distraction.

But it was an election year and small-town constituents had old-school values. They would frown on him dating a younger woman, especially a single mom. And that meant he'd have to keep things purely professional.

"How does this weekend sound?"

She looked up at him and heard her say, "Perfect," but saw on her face that she thought it was anything but, and he knew how she felt, but for a whole other reason.

Chapter Three

There were times you did things for your kid that you didn't really want to do. At least, that's what Lauren thought as she drove toward Bren's house later that week. She supposed she should be grateful Kyle wouldn't be climbing aboard a half-crazed animal today. He would just be learning some of the basics, Bren had explained.

Lauren glanced at her son. He had the same look on his face as he did staring at a pile of birthday presents: eyes wide, shoulders taut, upper body leaning forward, the freckles on his face standing out like specks of dirt. She loved those freckles even though he got them from his dad. The rest of her son—hair, eyes, jaw—that was all her.

"Are we there yet?" he asked, completely oblivious to her study.

She almost laughed. "Looks like it."

When she slowed down for Bren's driveway, he rested a hand on the door frame, peering at Bren's ranch house with anticipation in his eyes. She took in his home, too.

Nice place.

Being town sheriff must pay well. Of course, it was

nothing compared to her brother's ostentatious, obnoxiously huge, over-the-top mansion, but this was nice and in many ways more her style. Dark brown paint covered a single-story home that had a cute porch across the front and wide dormers poking out of the A-frame roofline. It was in the heart of town, other homes and corrals off in the distance making her think this was some sort of equestrian subdivision. All the homes in the area were evenly spaced apart, but while those homes featured white fencing, Bren's was made out of some sort of metal piping that looked sturdy enough to house elephants. There were trucks parked out front, and standing outside near the front of them, Bren and a group of men. He waved as Lauren wedged herself into a parking spot.

Kyle shot out of his seat before she put her compact car in Park.

"Hey!"

But he was gone, his door slamming shut, Kyle going up to Bren and the men gathered there. She saw him laugh and pat Kyle's head before pointing him somewhere. Her son waved and ran off, presumably to the back of the house and to the barn that she'd spotted out back.

Here goes.

She slipped out, smiling and shielding her eyes from the sun. "Should I follow him around?"

In answer, Bren beckoned her over, continuing his conversation with the three older cowboys. "Lauren, this is Andrew, Jim and George. They're part of my campaign committee."

Only then did she notice one of the trucks was black with a gold sheriff's star on the side. Bren rested a hand on the hood, the black shirt he wore sporting the same image.

"Guys, Lauren's new to the area," he said.

"Nice to meet you," said Andrew and Jim, smiling. Andrew was much older than Bren, his shoulders stooped, his blue eyes still bright. Jim seemed nearer in age. The two of them said, "Welcome," at almost the same time.

"Thanks."

George hadn't taken his eyes off her, and then he turned to Bren, and there was something about the look on his face that Lauren didn't like. Sort of a "well, well, well…what have we here?" He was older, too, but that didn't stop him from winking at Bren just before saying, "Now I see why you agreed to help the son."

She drew up sharply. Bren frowned. "Her kid's why I'm helping. Get your mind out of the gutter, George."

The man guffawed and Lauren sure hoped he was better at raising money than he was at handling social situations.

"I can just drop Kyle off if you want," Lauren told Bren.

He shook his head. "No, don't do that."

She'd planned to leave, but something about the look in George's eyes made her want to stay, even though a part of her, like, really super-duper wanted to escape.

"The boys are all around back, if you want to join them."

"Thanks." She smiled at the men. "Nice meeting you."

Not you, she telegraphed to George, but he was too busy making faces at Bren. Old fool.

She walked off with her head held high, turning her attention to the boys surrounding her son. They stood in front of a barn that matched the house and they were like cloned images of each other. They all wore jeans and Western shirts—some solid, some stripped—and cowboy hats that were either black or tan. They all wore leather belts, too, some with sparkling new buckles, others without, and dusty old cowboy boots. Most were older than her son, but they seemed welcoming even as they stared at her curiously.

Yes, I'm the overprotective mom, she silently told them.

"Sorry about that," Brennan said, coming to stand beside her.

"It's okay," she said over the sound of trucks starting up out front. "How's the campaign going, by the way?"

"Pretty good," he said. "Of course, you never know." He set off toward the barn. She hung back. "Gather around, boys." Bren motioned with a hand for the kids to join him inside the barn. "Last week we were working on finding our center. Anyone want to tell Kyle what that is?"

From town sheriff to bull-riding instructor. He handled the transition well.

One of the kids, a young teenager clearly going through puberty judging by the acne on his face, stepped forward. "It's when you're the middle and the bull spins around you." The kid made bucking movements with his hand. "Or beneath you while you stay perfectly center."

Bren smiled at the boy and Lauren noticed that he had a great smile. The kind that lit up his eyes and made the corners of them wrinkle and sparked the gold.

"That's right." That smile landed on her son and she found herself leaning against the back of the house.

"Kyle, you need to work on that a little more. I noticed at the rodeo the other day that you came out of the chutes leaning forward. Anyone want to tell Kyle why you don't do that?"

Another kid raised his hand. "Because once the bull starts moving, it's hard to get back to center."

"Exactly."

Suddenly she was staring into those gorgeous eyes, the smile on his face slipping away as their gazes connected, making her wonder what was wrong. She hated the way he made her feel as if she should check her appearance in a mirror, so much so that she self-consciously scanned the fancy jeans she'd donned for the occasion, the kind with rhinestones on the pockets. She wore a blousy shirt. It concealed her figure and hid her curves. She'd even put her hair into pigtails, for some reason feeling the need to play down her looks around Bren, and yet the way his smile faded made her skin catch fire and wonder what she'd done wrong.

"Today we're going to work on helping Kyle find his center, if that's okay with you, Mom."

A dozen eyes turned in her direction and her face grew even more red. "Of course."

What was with her? The man just asked a question. So what if he didn't act all friendly-like while he was teaching. No need to feel as if she'd been put on the witness stand and he was judge and jury.

"Who wants to work the controls today?"

A chorus of "Me! Me!" erupted from the kids. She looked around for these so-called controls, but there weren't any that she could see. She understood in a second when four of the boys broke apart from the group and headed toward the ropes that suspended a barrel off the ground. It was some sort of…ride. One of them even went into an empty stall and pulled out a mat of some sort, a fabric-covered piece of foam her son would land upon.

Oh, dear goodness.

She took half a step forward before stopping herself. This was her problem, she admitted. This right here. This overwhelming need to protect Kyle all the time. Of course, that was a mother's job—to keep her child safe from harm. But even she recognized she was a little out of control in that department. She freaked about him wearing a seat belt. She hated when he rode rides at carnivals. She refused to let him play in the ocean. And she wanted to vomit every time they went to the water park and she was forced to watch him slide into one of those little plastic tubes that spat him out on the other end. For some insane reason, she always worried he'd drop into some sort of water-ride black hole and never come out again.

Stupid. But it was because of *him*.

She didn't want to think about him. About the man who'd stolen her heart and then broken it into a million pieces.

It's in the past.

Because Kyle was her future and damned if she'd let Paul ruin her life all over again.

"Climb on aboard here, son."

Her chin tipped up. She forced herself to lean back again, even crossed her arms and made herself watch, one of her pigtails sliding over a shoulder.

You should leave.

No. She wasn't ready to do that yet. So she watched as Kyle raced up to the dark green barrel and Bren's smile slid back on his face. She could tell the man loved her son's enthusiasm and that he approved of his eagerness to learn. She wondered why he didn't have any kids of his own. What had stopped a good-looking man—as in a seriously *hot* older man—from settling down and having children? What was his story? Then again, maybe there was a Mrs. Bren Connelly inside the house. Crap. She hadn't even thought to ask.

"The first thing I want to see is how you take a wrap," she heard him say to her son.

And so what if there was a Mrs. Connelly? It wasn't as if she would ever consider dating the man. Yeah, he was handsome in an older-sexy-ranch-hand kind of way, but that wasn't her type. She preferred the more bookish type of men, like the men she went to school with—the kind that didn't like to deal with loaded guns. Besides, it was clear Bren didn't like her. Every time their gazes connected, his smile faded. Not a big fan of hers, clearly.

"Where'd you learn how to do that?" he asked Kyle.

Kyle sat on the barrel even though she didn't recall him climbing aboard. He smiled up at Bren in a way that flipped her stomach for another reason.

"I watched a video on YouTube," he announced.

She forced herself to pay attention. He had, indeed, watched videos. Tons of them. That's how she'd known he was serious about this whole steer-riding thing. It'd taken her weeks to admit to herself that nothing she said to dissuade him from the idea would work. It was her brother who'd stepped in and made her admit the truth. If she couldn't keep the Bubble Wrap on him his whole life, she might as well embrace his enthusiasm. She needed to let him go. If she kept him off steers, he'd find something else to do, Jax had warned, and he might not ask her permission the next time. That more than anything had scared her. Jax was right. Too tight a rein might push him to bolt, and so here they were.

"In for a penny, in for a pound," she muttered as Bren looked up and caught her eyes again. Something about the way he kept doing that prompted her to move forward, despite telling herself to stay back and give them both some space.

He didn't like her, or he didn't like something about her, and darned if she would let that keep her away.

And so she didn't.

DON'T COME OVER. Don't come over. Do not come over.
She pushed away from the back of the house.
Bren tried not to groan. And stare. And gawk.
Damn that George.

He'd been doing just fine at ignoring how gorgeous Lauren was right up until George made a fuss about her looks. Now he couldn't get her looks off his mind, either. He even had to blink a few times to get her out of his head. What was he saying…?

"The only thing I'd like to see you change is maybe how tight you wrap the rope around your hand," He glanced up and against his better judgment stared in her direction again. She was, indeed, headed this way.

Focus.

The bull rope—a prickly hemp tool that served as a bull rider's lifeline—came back into focus. "YouTube can't teach you the feel for how much pressure to use when you pull tight. It's like this. Here." Two of the boys stepped back as he went to work. "Do this."

He pulled, getting the thing tight around Kyle's hand. The boy's eager eyes watched his every move and for a moment he forgot about the kid's mother and how sexy she looked in her tight jeans and pigtails. Pigtails! They made her seem about twenty years younger than him— and served as a reminder of the age gap between them.

"I get it," Kyle said. "Not so tight that my hand tingles."

"Exactly."

He caught a whiff of her, and she smelled as good as fresh waffles on a Sunday morning. Sweet and with just a hint of vanilla.

"So if you're ready, I'm going to have the boys here start pulling on the ropes real good. It's going to get kind of hard to stay on, but that's okay, right, boys?"

The kids nodded, their faces eager, too. There was nothing they liked better than trying to knock each other off the barrel. He just hoped Lauren didn't freak out. Once glance at her face told him all he needed to know about how much she liked the idea of her son riding that barrel.

She should find her son another hobby, he thought. That would make *both* their lives easier.

"Ready?"

Hazel eyes looked up at him with complete determination. The kid had more freckles than a spotted trout, but the resolve in his gaze made him seem older. For the first time Bren wondered if Kyle was the real deal, something he'd only ever seen rarely, a kid who really wanted it. He didn't do it for the bulls or the glory but because he was drawn to it.

Like he himself had been once upon a time.

"Go!" he told his students.

One tugged down, another sideways, and one pulled a rope toward him. Poor Kyle didn't know what hit him.

One moment he sat in the middle of the barrel; the next he was flat on the safety mat.

"Kyle!" Lauren called.

"I'm fine, Mom." Kyle sat up so quick Bren could tell he did so for his mother's sake. It was his grin that told him that he wasn't hurt. Not in the least. His eyes had lit up like an ocean sunrise. "Can I do it again?"

Bren pulled his gaze away from Lauren. At least she'd stopped short of bending down by her son's side. She must have spotted the brief warning in Kyle's eyes, the one that had clearly said, *Don't humiliate me, Mom.*

"I'm not sure that's a good idea." Lauren glanced at Bren as if seeking his help to convince her son, but he shook his head.

"He needs to do it again. Had this been a real steer, he would have hurt himself coming off like that, especially since he'd be landing on hard ground." He glanced down at Kyle, who already stood up. "You can't put your arms out like that. Don't try and land on your feet. Don't stick a limb out in front of you. And most importantly, never land on your head." He nodded toward the barrel. "Do it again."

Lauren didn't exactly gulp, but she did something close. Worried eyes caught his own and even though he told himself to keep things cool between them, he smiled. He just wanted to reassure her. To let her know nothing would happen, not on his watch, but seeing the way she relaxed, watching her take a deep breath and then ever so slightly smile back... It was his turn to gulp.

"Don't forget to wrap it tighter."

Kyle nodded absently as he climbed back on board.

"Look where you want to fall," one of the other kids

told him. Michael was his name. Good kid without a lick of talent, but he sure tried hard, and Bren appreciated the way he wanted to help.

"Curl into a ball if you come off headfirst," said another one. Perry, his neighbor's kid, who rode steers more because of the girls it attracted than any real love of the sport.

"But don't stop trying," Rhett advised.

It filled him with pride. This was why he did what he did. He might not ride bulls anymore. He might be all washed up. But he still knew things that he could pass on to kids who wanted to learn.

"Ready?" he asked Kyle when he was all settled. The boy nodded again, throwing his hand up in the air this time as if he rode a real bull, and Bren tried not to smile. He glanced at Rhett and nodded, and the chaos began all over again. Kyle tipped left, but darned if he didn't correct himself this time. Same thing happened the other way, but he hung on, for a little while at least, because one of the kids jerked the rope so hard it looked like Kyle rode a trampoline. He heard Lauren gasp as her son flew right, hand hanging up on the rope for a moment, arms flailing as he landed on the right side of the mat with a whoosh. He'd listened, too, because he'd curled his arms up tight. Bren smiled because a lot of kids couldn't think that fast. The adrenaline, the fear, it all got to them. Clearly Kyle could slow down his mind. He could think. And he loved it, because he smiled the whole time.

Lauren, not so much.

She sat there staring at her son, leaning forward, perched on the tips of her toes, as if she were about to launch herself at him.

"You need to work on your balance more."

"Ride horses," Rhett said, helping Kyle up. "If you have any."

Kyle turned toward his mom. "My uncle Jax has a ton of horses."

"I bet your uncle would have some great horses for you to ride," Bren said.

"Riding will help *a lot*," said another of his students.

"He doesn't know how to ride," said Lauren, and he could tell she didn't like the idea of Kyle riding a horse any more than she liked the thought of him on a steer.

"Bren can teach him," said Rhett. "Bren used to ride broncs and bulls."

"He's been to the NFR," Perry added.

"A long time ago," Bren told her. "Right after I got out of the army."

"I know," Kyle said, hopping off the mat and standing next to his mother. "My uncle said you got some kind of special accommodation in the army. Is that true?"

"A Distinguished Service Cross," he admitted.

"That's cool," Kyle said.

Something in Lauren's eyes flickered, and it wasn't approval. It was more like…disappointment, and that was so completely opposite to the usual reaction that the realization kind of threw him to the point he found himself saying, "I'd be happy to teach Kyle to ride," before he could think better of it.

"That's okay." She shook her head, pigtails waving behind her. "My brother has a qualified instructor coming to teach at his ranch."

"Mom, that's not for weeks. Uncle Jax told you that just yesterday."

"Then you'll have to wait."

Kyle caught his eyes. "I can teach myself, can't I?"

"No, you can't," his mom immediately replied hotly.

"It's really no problem." Although why Bren argued, he had no idea. He should let her have her way. Take her side. He found her pigtails entirely too adorable, not to mention his curiosity was now peaked. What was her deal with former military personnel? Because it was clear she had an issue with them.

Or maybe it was just him?

"Kyle would learn how to ride a lot faster if I helped out," he added. "I can teach principles that will cross over into bull riding."

"He can," echoed Perry.

"Come on, Mom. I'm entered in that rodeo next month. I don't have time to wait for Uncle Jax's riding person to arrive."

Bren crossed his arms and gave her the same stare he'd given some of his subordinates when they were thinking of doing something they shouldn't. "Of course, if you want to risk his safety..."

She knew he manipulated her. The disapproval in her gaze deepened and he told himself that was good. He didn't want her approval. He wanted her to keep her distance.

At least, that's what he told himself, because when she straightened and her chin flicked up and her pretty hazel eyes sparked and she said, "All right, fine," there was a part of him that did the same thing Kyle did.

"Yessss!" the kid yelled.

Chapter Four

She should have said no.

You're just nervous about Kyle learning how to ride.

But she knew it wasn't just that. It was *him*. Bren Connelly. The former Green Beret. Gosh darn it all, another testosterone-filled male in her life. Just what she needed. He reminded her of Paul. And why not? They had both been manufactured at the same war-machine factory.

Too bad.

She would never go down that road again. Never, never, never. Which was really a shame because she'd found him kind of attractive.

Kind of?

Okay, very.

She heard his truck before she spotted it. For a moment she wished Kyle were with her, but he'd gone down to the stables ahead of her with Jax. The two were saddling up the horse they would use today, and so it was just her.

Don't be afraid.

Bren was *not* Paul.

Besides, Bren was so aloof. He had no romantic interest in her. He wouldn't wine and dine and woo her and then…change. Bren hardly glanced her way. That was good. She needed to keep it that way. She forced a wide smile on her face and pulled open her front door. At least he'd followed her instructions. She told him to drive around to the side of the house, to where the guest's quarters of her brother's multimillion-dollar home were located.

"Wow."

That was all he said when he stepped out of the same black Dodge truck she'd seen at his house. The vehicle matched his all-black outfit right down to the cowboy hat. Not that she expected a warm greeting from him or anything. Ever since that first day he'd been so…stand-offish. Still, a "Hi" or a "Hello" or "Good to see you" would have been nice. Not that she really blamed him. Her brother's home could make a politician speechless.

"It's kind of over the top, isn't it?"

Bren had completely ignored her words, just stood in place, tipped his hat back, topaz-colored eyes taking it all in. She'd done the same thing when she'd first arrived.

The house had been built into the side of a hill, one covered by oak trees and a small outcropping of rocks. It'd been designed by some bigwig mucky-muck in New York, one who specialized in feng shui. Her brother believed in luck and Karma and all that other crazy stuff, so she hadn't been surprised that he'd built his monstrous-sized home out of "natural elements," in this case redwood and granite, and then ordered it to blend in with its surroundings. Three stories tall, it boasted a steep roof in the middle and two smaller peaks on the left and right. Giant beams stuck out at the ends, a design mimicked around the ranch. The second and third floors both opened up to decks, but she lived on the bottom floor, around the side, which sounded not as nice but, in fact, was super spacious and comfortable, and she thanked God for the roof over her head every day.

"And you live there?" He pointed behind her.

She followed his gaze, remembering what she'd thought when she'd seen the private entrance. She had a deck, too, although hers was more like a porch, the narrow steps leading to a door with windows on either side of it. Her apartment might look like a tiny portion of her brother's giant mansion, but that wasn't the case at all. She had the entire corner of the house—and given the size of that home, that said a lot—plus three bedrooms and a kitchen that overlooked the backyard. Even though the home had been nestled against the side of a hill, it was really more of an illusion. They had carved away the hillside to make room for more decking and a pool, all of which she could spy from her kitchen and family room windows along the back of her apartment.

"It's supposed to be the maid's quarters." She'd laughed when she heard that. Her brother—with a maid. "But he's letting me and Kyle live here until I'm back on my feet."

Because her life had completely fallen apart when Paul had died. The lies. The half-truths. It had all come to a head and she'd been forced to pick up the pieces of her shattered heart and start all over again. And she'd been doing fine, too. She'd raised Kyle while holding down a job and going to school at night. But then Jax had visited her. His visits had been so few and far between when he'd been working full time. But now he wasn't, and he'd seen the hovel where she lived and had insisted she move into his new place. It had meant moving to a different city and rebuilding their lives from scratch, but she'd done it for Kyle. He'd been happier than she'd ever seen him and it made her hope he'd escaped her marriage to Paul unscathed.

"Where's the riding stables?" His gaze scanned the perimeter.

"Out back."

He appeared skeptical. She didn't blame him. The first day they'd driven up to her brother's new home, right after she'd picked her jaw up off the floor— pictures did not do the mansion justice—Kyle had asked the same question. Surrounded by trees and the hillside, it didn't appear to be anything other than just a home out in the middle of nowhere.

"It's hidden," she said.

Right then, as if on cue, a horse nickered in the distance. Bren turned toward the sound coming from the tree-studded hillside and cocked his head.

"It's around on the other side." She pointed to a gravel road that swept past her apartment and wound through the hills. "Kyle's already down there."

He nodded, but whereas last week he'd pretty much ignored her, today he turned and studied her. She felt the urge to brush a hand through her hair. She'd left it down today. No more pigtails, but for some reason she wished she'd taken time to style it a little more.

Stupid. *Former Green Beret, remember?*

"I heard your brother is a military contractor." He cocked his head a bit as he awaited her answer.

"He was," she said, glancing down at her new boots. They weren't broken in yet and they already hurt. "He's mostly retired now. Focusing on Hooves for Heroes."

Because far be it from Jax to retire, although she supposed that at thirty-eight, he was far too young for that. Still, most men in his position would want to travel the world, to forget the past and the stress of their previous line of work. Not her brother. No. He wanted to help the men and women who'd served their country—and had the scars to prove it.

"If you don't mind driving, we can go down there now, unless you're not supposed to drive civilians around in your vehicle or something."

"I won't exactly be driving on city streets." He shot her a smile. "Not that it matters. The truck's a perk of the job. I can do whatever I want with it."

Must be nice, she thought. But she supposed a lawman was never really off duty, and so who was she to pass judgment?

"It's just a little too far to walk," she said, "and my brother already took off with the Rhino."

There he went studying her again. Why, oh why, did she feel her skin begin to prickle, her fair flesh no doubt changing colors like a neon sign behind a window. It was as if he knew she had a secret.

"The Rhino is an all-terrain vehicle Jax bought to drive back and forth to the stable area," she explained because she felt the need to say *something*.

"I know what a Rhino is."

Then why did he stare at her so intently? She almost asked the question. Instead she swallowed, looking toward his truck. "Is it unlocked?"

In response he moved to the passenger side of his truck and opened it. She hadn't had a man open the door for her in, well, a long, long time.

"Thanks."

He smiled. She had to look away.

Great. Less than two minutes in his company and it was all she could do to look him in the eye. He made her edgy. Made her mouth go dry at the mere thought of sitting next to him for a quick jaunt to the stables. He caused her heart to beat what felt like a million beats per minute.

"Need help up?" he asked, holding out a supporting hand.

"No, I'm fine."

She'd never been inside a law enforcement vehicle before, and so she told herself that was why she hesitated to get inside. There was a gun on a rack in between the seat and a computer on a stand attached to the dash. But she knew that wasn't why she paused. It was because she was suddenly…afraid.

Why?

He must have thought she couldn't make it up on her own, because he helped her anyway, his hand capturing the crook of her elbow and gently guiding her. She might have moved, but inside, everything froze, her breathing, her heart, even her vision as she stared straight ahead. And then he let her go and she wilted into the cab of his truck, the door sealing with a pop.

Oh, dear Lord.

How would she ever make it through the next few hours?

SHE'D GONE QUIET on him. That was okay. They didn't need to get chatty, or even friendly, not if he wanted to keep his distance—which he did, he reminded himself. George's reaction the other day had been all the proof he needed that she was too young for him. The man had razzed him right up until the moment he'd walked away. And if he needed further proof, he'd done some checking around. Knew for a fact that she was twelve years his junior. Too young. When he'd been eighteen, she'd been six. Hell, when he'd been in combat, she'd been in high school. It had just felt wrong to notice how attractive she'd looked standing there in her tight jeans and a white T-shirt that clung to her body. Wrong and yet oh so right.

"There it is."

It took her words to shake him out of his reverie, to look ahead and damn near slam on the brakes. A barn had come into view, although calling it a barn was like calling the White House a home. It wasn't just a stable; it appeared to be an arena and stable combined, one with a steep angled roof and large wooden beams poking out from the side just like the main house.

"Exactly how rich is your brother?"

"I know." She shot him a tight smile. "It's massive, isn't it?"

And it only grew bigger as they approached. It'd been built in the middle of a meadow, one framed by redwood fence posts, horses grazing in the distance. It was a covered arena, he noted, but clearly taller than any he'd seen before, and he realized why as they drew closer. He could see windows inset into the long side, not the type used to allow light into the interior but large panes of glass trimmed with dark-stained wood. The exterior of the place was all wood, too. No metal beams in sight like most big-time arenas. Amazing didn't begin to describe the place. Even the short side of the arena, something that was usually kept open, had been closed off, cathedral-sized windows stretching toward the top, smaller on the short side and then getting bigger toward the middle.

"Are those apartments along the top?" he asked, having spotted walls through the side windows.

She nodded. "Both sides, actually. Four in all. They're for guests."

He'd never seen anything like it. But what a great idea. Judging by the size of the arena, the apartments must be huge and, he would bet, every bit as luxurious as the main residence.

"Do you have anybody living in them?" He didn't see any cars parked out front. The place seemed completely deserted, so if her son was inside, he couldn't tell. The only sign of life was the Rhino parked out front, the vehicle stopped at an odd angle. He pulled up next to it.

"Not yet." She glanced over at him, but it was quick, her hazel eyes catching his gaze for a moment before she looked away. She was like a shy kitten, one that wanted to be friendly but didn't quite trust the human next to her. "Kyle should be inside. They're getting a horse ready to ride."

There was an entrance on one side of the barn with double doors and the initials HFH carved above it, and she slipped out of the truck and headed toward it. Hooves for Heroes. A sign stood next to the door. He silently whistled as they stepped inside, and if he were honest with himself, he half expected a red carpet on the other side. Instead there were more big beams stretching up toward the crown of the roof, the same beams that poked through the sides. It really was like a cathedral, he thought, pausing to get his bearings. Sunlight filtered in through windows in the roof. Tiny motes of dust danced in the beams of light, the particles seeming to swirl through the air. No need for artificial lighting in here, at least not during the day. The smell of freshly stained wood mixed with the pine and Bren knew they must have just completed construction a short time ago.

"Mom!"

Her son had slipped out of a stall, or maybe a grooming area—they were too far away to tell—his short legs pumping as he ran down the aisle.

"Hey," he warned. "No running in the barn. You might spook the horses."

He still couldn't believe this was anything resembling a barn. The boy skidded to a stop, a wide smile on his face.

"Uncle Jax is in with Rowdy, but we're having a little trouble with the saddle." Brown eyes just like his mom's peered up at him. "Thank goodness you're here. YouTube has been no help."

For some reason, the words almost made him laugh. Was everything YouTube-able these days? The kid turned and started to run back the way he'd come, caught himself and walked, but his steps were just shy of a jog, he was so full of enthusiasm and eager anticipation, and it made him want to smile and point out to Lauren how lucky she was that she'd found her son's passion so early in life. He didn't. She would barely look at him today and it had him wondering yet again what had happened to her. No amount of poking around had helped. She was too new to the area. He'd resisted the urge to snoop around online, too. Or use his resources at work. Whatever it was that had turned her kind eyes into pools of uncertainty, he would find out…in time.

They reached what was clearly a grooming stall. Bren would have gone inside except he drew up short at the sight that greeted him. Bren had seen some pretty remarkable things during his tenure as sheriff, hilarious things, and so he somehow held it together. What he wanted to do was double over in laughter. The horse's halter was on upside down. They'd gotten the nose part right, but the leather strip that was supposed to run beneath the chin and throatlatch stretched instead up the middle of the horse's face like some kind of medieval headstall. The halter should have buckled up by the horse's ear, too, but the brass fitting must have been on the other side, down by the throat. The cross ties were attached to the rings by the neck, not the ones by the horse's nose. And the saddle was on, but they'd used a back cinch for the front and the front girth for the back, although how they'd managed to do that when they had different fittings was anybody's guess. But perhaps the most comical thing of all was the look on the sorrel horse's face. It had such a pained expression of "help me" in its eyes that it was all Bren could do to hold it together.

"What's wrong?" Lauren asked.

"Well," he said, tipping his cowboy hat back. "It's hard to know where to start."

Chapter Five

"This is why you need to hire somebody to manage the horses," Lauren said, standing back and watching Bren fix the horse's halter. "And to think, I was going to have you help Kyle ride the other day."

"Yeah, good thing I got sick," Kyle said.

"I already *did* hire somebody," Jax said, hands on his hips. "She won't be here until next month. I told you."

"Thank goodness I didn't ride him that day," Kyle said. He stood at Bren's elbow, intently observing everything the man did. "I could have been killed."

"Judging by how this horse tolerated everything, I doubt that." Bren stood back, and she hated the way her cheeks heated up when he turned to face her. Well, turned to face her and her brother. It was just embarrassment, she told herself, although she'd had nothing to do with getting the horse ready to ride.

"How are you going to manage a horseback-riding program when you don't even know how to put a saddle on?"

The look on her brother's face was one she recognized from her childhood. Stubbornness and determination. She remembered the look from when he tried putting together a new set of Legos. "I know how to put one on."

"Yeah, *now*," her son said.

Jax just shook his head in that way he had. He might be ten years her senior, but they'd had plenty of tussles in their youth. They'd usually involved the television remote or his computer games, but this was no different from the time she told him not to steal their dad's car keys. Her brother had never been able to take criticism well, which was part of the reason why he'd been so successful in the military and then later when he'd started his own private contracting firm. He was a take-charge kind of guy, even when what he was in charge of was something completely unfamiliar.

"I'm just glad Bren came over before something happened."

Jax shot her an impatient glare, but before he could say a word, Bren interjected with, "You ready to learn how to ride?"

Her son's enthusiastic "Yes!" startled not just her but the horse, too, the animal lifting its head, eyes wide.

"Okay, so that's lesson number one." Bren tossed her son a smile, one that made her insides do something strange, and that reminded her of the way Paul used to look at him...before. "Don't yell around horses."

Okay, don't think about Paul.

She inhaled sharply, her emotions too close to the surface. "Thank Bren for teaching you to saddle up a horse."

"Thank you, Bren," her brother said in a singsong voice that made her want to elbow him in the side. Her son glanced back at his uncle and smiled.

"Thanks," Kyle said. "Although I really wish I was riding a steer."

"In time." Bren patted her son on the head and that made her go all mushy all over again. Goodness, what was wrong with her? It'd been four years since Paul's death. Four long years of waking up in the middle of the night, scared to death. Of waiting for him to call, only to realize he never would again. Of hearing a car pull up and going tense inside and then recognizing that it wasn't Paul and that he wasn't coming home and feeling such a rush of relief coupled with guilt and horror that she could feel that way. Lord, how she wished she could get over that. She'd been hoping the move would help. It hadn't.

She felt her brother's gaze on her. The two of them had gotten close since her husband's death, probably in part because Paul used to work for her brother. She had a feeling Jax knew everything about her and Paul. All of it, which explained his insistence that she move in with him.

"Do you know how to lead a horse?" she heard Bren ask, the man so much like Paul and yet so different. Or maybe not. They all started out nice at first. History was littered with the bodies of women who'd been suckered in by a sweet smile and a bouquet of roses.

"Sure," her son said confidently, taking the reins from Bren's hands and tugging the horse forward.

"No, not like that," he said as the horse planted its feet, neck stretched out in response to her son pulling on the reins. "You need to get back by his head. Walk alongside of him. Ask him nicely to follow you with your hands."

But Bren had more patience than Paul ever had. He smiled at her son, and if she were honest, she could admit she liked the smile. It seemed filled with kind-ness and a genuine desire to help.

"Maybe I should be in on all this training," she heard her brother mutter.

"Maybe you should," Bren echoed.

"You should take lessons, too," her brother said to her.

"What?"

Bren must have heard Jax, because he'd paused, and she could feel his gaze on her and it made her want to turn away, to face her brother and place her hands on her hips and demand, *What were you thinking?*

"You need to learn how to handle horses," he said with a smile.

"Why would I need to learn that?"

"You totally should, Mom," Kyle said. "That way you could help out around here."

Her brother's smile grew. "Exactly."

She shot her sibling a glare because her brother knew how she felt about horses. They were too big. Too... smelly. Too...scary.

"No, thank you. I have enough to do, what with school and finding a job and raising a son. Or have you forgotten that I've got one more semester before I gradu-ate as a registered nurse? I plan to work for a hospital, not a horse hotel."

"It's a therapeutic ranch," Jax corrected.

"And it's a beauty, but I'm not taking horse lessons."

"What if there's a fire?" They all turned toward Bren. "Or a natural disaster," he added. "What if you're needed in the barn for some reason?"

She let out a breath she hadn't even known she'd been holding. He had changed. Or something in his eyes had changed. He no longer stared at her like a dog would a porcupine. Instead he stared at her in a way that made her skin flush. As if he had tried to pry open her head and see inside.

"The odds of me ever getting near a horse are slim to nil."

"You don't like them?" Bren asked.

"I much prefer dogs."

His eyes took on the glint of a gold coin in the sun. "That's too bad."

Why? she wondered. Why was it too bad? What did he care if she liked horses or not?

"Well, I think I should hire you. At least until my new hippotherapist arrives."

"Jax, the man already has a job. He doesn't need another one, I'm sure."

"Actually, I'd love to help out."

That made her head whip around so fast she temporarily blinded herself with her hair. "You don't have to do that."

"No. It's okay, but I have a favor to ask in return."

Her brother eyed Bren expectantly. "Name it."

"I do some volunteer work down at the VA and I know someone who could really benefit from a program like this. Any chance I could bump his name to the top of your guest list?"

"You got it," Jax said. "Frankly, we're so new we don't even have one yet, but your friend is first."

Bren came forward, hand outstretched. "Deal."

And that was when Lauren knew she'd be seeing a heck of a lot more of Bren than she wanted to.

BREN SPENT AN HOUR working with her son, an hour during which Lauren stood off to the side and watched. Her

brother didn't seem to mind helping out. He acted as
spotter when Bren started Kyle on trotting. Jax wasn't
afraid to dive in and work, something he admired
about the man. He didn't act like someone with a pile
of money, either, and that impressed Bren, too. There
were two types of people in the world: those who had
money and liked to let everyone know it, and those
who had money and kept their humility. Jax Stone was
the latter.

"You getting sore up there, buddy?" Bren asked as
the dust the horse kicked up settled around them. It
was getting dark, not that it mattered. He was sure the
place had lights.

"I'm fine."

That's what he said, but Bren knew differently.
They'd been working him pretty hard. He'd taught the
kid the distinction between sitting on an animal and
actually moving as one with a horse. He'd taught him
signs to look for in not just a horse but a steer, too. A
tipped head gave clues as to what direction an animal
would take. Ears could indicate anger or fear or interest. Animals communicated in a hundred different
ways if someone just took the time to pay attention,
and it was that type of knowledge that could help you
in competition.

"He won't quit unless you tell him to stop," Lauren
said quietly.

They leaned against the wooden rail that surrounded
the arena. He'd turned Kyle loose a few minutes ago on
Rowdy. He didn't know who'd picked out the ranch's
livestock, but they'd selected a winner in Rowdy. The
horse was patient and kind and knew how to treat a
stone-cold beginner like Kyle. As for Jax, he'd taken off

a short while ago to answer his cell phone. It was just the three of them inside the massive space.

"I have a feeling he gets that from his mom."

She glanced up at him and he could tell she was no more comfortable around him now than she'd been a half hour ago. If anything, less so now that her brother was gone.

"His dad was stubborn, too."

And there it was again. The spark in her eyes. The one that flared for a second and then seemed to be snuffed out, almost as if her memories smothered it cold.

"I'm sorry about your loss."

The flash returned again, but there was something more than just a flash. Was it anger? Sadness? Disappointment? Whatever, it was something that made him lean forward a bit as he waited for her response.

But all she said was "Thank you."

That wasn't what she'd wanted to say. He would bet his life on it.

He stared at her son, the boy catching his glance and grinning from ear to ear. "Must be tough raising a kid on your own."

Her hands clutched the rail in front of her, blanching the knuckles and turning the tips of her fingers bright red. "You have no idea."

No. He didn't. He'd never felt the urge to marry. He told himself it was because he hadn't found the right woman, but deep down, he knew the truth. He liked being single. He enjoyed his freedom. He liked to go wherever he wanted, whenever he wanted to do it, and so he respected people who, like Lauren, were willing to sacrifice such a huge part of themselves to raise another human being. Actually, respect didn't begin to cover what he felt.

"You did the right thing moving here." He had no idea why he said the words, but he knew he'd hit a nerve when she turned toward him. "It's a great place to raise kids."

She flicked her chin up. "Thank you for your approval."

And now she'd taken his words wrong. "I just meant a lot of people move here to raise kids. We have good schools and good people and a community spirit that's hard to beat."

"So says the sheriff that's up for reelection."

Did he sound like a politician? Man, this had gone from bad to worse. "I love my hometown."

He saw her take a deep breath, and it was as if she forced herself to relax, as if she reached for something deep inside her that would help her find her center. "I'm sorry." She clenched the wooden rail. "I'm just edgy when Kyle's around big animals."

Then she'd have a hell of a time when he started riding bulls, but he couldn't say that. He watched as she lowered her hands back to her sides.

"It's been a long day," she added.

"It's okay." He forced a smile. "You can make it up to me in the voter's booth."

She stared up at him with her big hazel eyes and the strangest thing happened. He felt himself tip toward her, as if she were a magnet and he were a piece of metal that couldn't fight the force that drew him to her.

Damn, he thought, making himself lean back. She must have felt it, too…whatever "it" was, because she turned away and called out, "Kyle, I think it's time to stop."

"But, Mo-om."

Jax returned then, instructing, "Do as your mother says."

Kyle nodded, reluctantly turning in their direction.

Jax asked, "How'd he do?"

"He did great," Bren answered, having to work to re-center himself, too. What the hell had just happened?

"I really want to keep going," Kyle said a moment later.

"It's time to call it quits. You still have homework to do," she added.

"And we need to eat dinner," the boy's uncle said.

"That, too." She looked at Bren and the chilliness was back in her eyes. "Thanks for coming out."

"When can we do it again?" Kyle asked, guiding the horse toward the rail with an ease that was impressive given he'd only ever ridden this one time.

"That's up to your mom," Bren said. Clearly the battle lines had been drawn again. That was okay. That was good, in fact, he told himself.

"Actually," Jax said with a glance at his sister, "it'd be great if you came out tomorrow. I'm told the horses need shoes and there's a farrier coming over tomorrow, but I don't have a clue about how that works."

"Sure," he said. "I'll come over after my shift is done."

"Does that mean I can ride again tomorrow?"

"Sounds like it," Lauren said, seeming to be anything but pleased.

"And as a thank-you, why don't you stay for dinner

tonight? I don't cook a whole lot, but I make a pretty good pizza," Jax said.

"Uncle Jax has a brick oven."

Bren raised an eyebrow.

Kyle nodded so fast it was a wonder he didn't get dizzy. "It's super cool."

He glanced at Lauren to see how she took the request and almost laughed at the glint of dismay he spotted in her eyes. But like a page being scrubbed by a pencil eraser, her face cleared and she even managed a smile. "My brother's being modest. He's definitely the cook in the family."

"Comes with being in the service," Jax said.

And there it went again. The light in her eyes. Snuffed. He'd been staring right at her when it happened, and so he knew that he wasn't mistaken and that it had something to do with him.

"Come on over," Jax said. "Lauren, you should come over, too, tonight."

"Oh, no." She shook her head emphatically. "Boys' night, remember? I'm studying. You two go on."

"You need to eat, too, Mom."

"You can bring me a piece after."

"No," said Jax. "You're coming over and that's that. Decision made."

"Jax—"

"Otherwise we'll bring the pizza party to you."

Bren watched her shoulder sag like a disappointed child. "I really need to study."

"Like Kyle said, you need to eat, too."

"I really do have to study."

"Just a half hour."

She tipped her head back and sighed, "Fine."

"Yeaaaaaah!" Kyle said. "Family night. Plus, I can show Bren my collection of bull-rider action figures."

But Lauren turned and walked away, tossing over her shoulder, "I'll see you at the house."

Her brother caught his eye, shrugged, mouthing, *Women.*

No. It was this one woman. She didn't like him, and damned if he didn't want to find out why.

Chapter Six

Dinner.

How in the heck would she get through that? The man made her as edgy as a cat in a room full of dogs. Bren Connelly was a damn fine-looking specimen, yes. She had no problem admitting that. After they'd left his house the other day, she'd found herself thinking about his topaz-colored eyes, how they were neither brown nor gold but some pale color between. Those eyes had held humor and warmth and understanding, and it was the latter that disturbed her the most.

He was good with kids, though. She would have to admit that, too. The patience in his voice soothed even her and she wondered what the story was with Sheriff Bren Connelly. Older, but handsome. She'd broken down and asked her brother if he was married. He wasn't. But she would bet the women of Via Del Caballo tried to pin him down. Was there a future Mrs. Connelly waiting in the wings?

Did it matter?

It didn't, she thought, letting herself inside her apartment. The place still smelled new—like freshly cut trees and lemon polish. And it was huge compared to her apartment back in San Jose. "We're supposed to head straight over to Uncle Jax's," Kyle said without so much as a hello, the door slamming closed behind him and Lauren's heart bouncing out of her chest in the process. She hadn't even heard the truck drive by. "He said to meet out by the pool."

"You can go now," she said, covering her heart with her hand. "I'll be up in just a minute."

That stopped the boy in his tracks. He seemed so much like Jax in that moment that it made her breath freeze all over again. She'd forgotten what he'd looked like at that age until that very moment, when her own son stared at her with her brother's eyes and with the same expression of gentle admonishment on his face as he'd had when she'd stolen his set of Legos.

"You're not going to bail on us, are you?"

He even sounded like Jax. Ten years going on thirty-eight.

"No. I just need a minute to pull my homework off the internet."

Hazel eyes narrowed as he squinted, almost as if he tried to examine her more closely to determine the truth in her words. It wasn't a lie. Not exactly.

"I'll tell them you'll be up in fifteen minutes." He turned and ran off toward his room, Lauren smiling at how adult he'd sounded. But then he completely spoiled the effect by emerging with an armful of tiny toy men. His bull-rider collection.

"See you up there."

Sigh. She supposed he would.

But first she really did have to print off her homework. Well, her assignment sheet. It'd take about two seconds.

She had to cross through the family room, passing

the kitchen off to her right and a breakfast nook that overlooked the backyard to her left, and head down a hall to her own ginormous room. Kyle had his own room, too.

"My own bed!" he'd cried when he'd first seen the place.

Nothing like your kid pointing out the shortcomings of your living situation to make you feel like a bad mom. They'd been sharing a room since Paul's death. She'd thought it'd been okay, but then Kyle had seen the apartment at her brother's ranch and he'd gone crazy and she'd known she'd have no choice but to take Jax up on his offer and move in with him. So she'd done it—for Kyle's sake, because she hated charity. Living off her brother's goodwill felt like the worst sort of hand out, as if she couldn't take care of herself and so she had to mooch off big brother.

She'd made it to her bedroom, she realized, but she stood in the middle of it, gazing off into nowhere. So she quickly opened her laptop, tapped keys and listened to the printer spitting out pages. Then she slowly sank onto her bed as she waited, a crazy thought occurring to her.

She was attracted to Bren.

As she'd stood next to him on the rail of that arena, watching him call out commands to her son, she'd been unable to deny it. Why she always went for the tall, dark and military type she had no idea. Maybe it was because she'd always admired her brother. It'd taken a bad marriage to make her realize some men could look like heroes on the outside and be anything but on the inside.

She got up and headed to her closet—a walk-in, no less; "Fancy," Kyle had said—and pulled a blouse off the rack to her left. It wasn't blingy or anything like that. Just a sheer top with a built-in chemise beneath. It hung loose around her upper arms, gathered by elastic at the crooks of her elbows. She resisted the urge to change out of her jeans, too. She didn't want him to think she cared about her appearance or anything. She just didn't want to look like a complete slob in her brother's glorious house.

That's what she told herself.

But as she headed out the front door and then around to the back of the house, she experienced something she hadn't felt since high school. The same flutter she'd felt when Paul Danners had walked into her homeroom. The same trill of excitement. The same sense of awareness. The same gut feeling that their futures were linked. If only it'd all turned out like a Cinderella story.

"And this one is Trent Anderson," Kyle was saying, holding up a tiny figurine and waving it in Bren's face. Her son sat on a thickly padded chair with a redwood frame that matched the covering on a patio that was bigger than her old apartment in the Bay Area. It didn't matter how often she visited her brother; the beauty of his home took her breath away. He had a pool, the kind found at a multimillion-dollar resort. Tonight the water sparkled, catching the last rays of the evening sun. But it wasn't the stunning surroundings that made her freeze. It was the sight of Kyle handing his precious toys to Bren.

"Trent Anderson?" Bren said, a laugh escaping from him that was both masculine and sexy at the same time. "Tell me it isn't so."

"It is." Kyle nodded emphatically. "Six-time NFR qualifier in bull riding. Did you know he was in a terrible accident that nearly destroyed his career? That they thought he'd never walk again, but then he went to a ranch like this one and they helped him recover?"

"I did know that." Bren stared down at the toy with a look of amused satisfaction. "I consider Trent one of my best friends."

"What?" Kyle practically bounced in his seat. "Are you *kidding* me?"

She forced herself to move forward. "Kyle, calm down. You about busted my ears with that shriek."

Her son turned and faced her. "Mom. Did you hear that? He knows Trent Anderson."

"Well, of course he does," she said, walking over to her brother, the pungent smell of fresh-cut basil and parsley filling the air. Her brother glanced up from his chopping and she detected amusement in his eyes. It was good to see. Usually he was so serious, but that was twice today she'd seen him relax a bit, both times around Bren.

"I'm doing a meat pizza for the boys," he said, patting his belly. "And a garden pizza for you."

That was the big brother she remembered from her childhood, always thinking about her. "Sounds good to me."

He went back to work and she took a deep breath, steeling herself as she faced Bren and her son. "I'm sure Bren knows a lot of famous bull riders."

Their gazes connected and there it went again. Whoosh. Her stomach did the same thing it did on the roller coasters she used to ride as a kid. It didn't make any sense, but she couldn't deny it.

"Do you?" Kyle's face peered up at him with such a look of unabashed awe Lauren smiled. She might want to avoid Bren like the plague, but clearly her kid had a big case of hero worship.

"I do."

"Like who?"

Kyle listened as Bren rattled off a bunch of names Lauren didn't recognize, but her son obviously did based on his "Really?" and "Wow!" and "No way!" Poor Kyle had had so little interaction with anyone who was hero material.

Including his own father.

She shoved that thought away with both hands. That was a lot of years ago.

She'd started over again.

In less than a year she'd be out of school. She'd find a job at one of the big hospitals and give her son all the things she'd dreamed about.

"...man, I would so love to meet him."

"You could." Bren glanced at her. "There's a big bull-riding event an hour away from here this weekend. You and your mom should go. I'll introduce you."

Wait...what?

"You should." Her brother sprinkled cheese on his creation. "Be good for the two of you to get out."

She told her brother with her eyes she didn't want to go, but instead of watching her back, her traitorous brother said, "I might like to go, too."

"Really, Uncle Jax?" Her son couldn't have sounded more excited if he'd been offered a chance to meet a Marvel superhero. "That'd be awesome."

She felt her mouth open and close a few times, caught her son's gaze, then Bren's. How could she say no?

"When is it again?" she asked, dreading his answer.

"Saturday?"

"Can we go, Mom?"

She swallowed. Hard. Did she have a choice?

LAUREN DIDN'T LOOK HAPPY.

"Thanks for the pizza," Bren said to Jax, stretching with the reach of someone well satisfied. "It was terrific."

"Thanks," Jax said gruffly, seeming uncomfortable with the praise.

"Kyle, come on." She wasted no time, that was for certain. "You need to get to bed. School tomorrow."

"But, Mom—"

She bit her lip and Bren enjoyed watching the way her teeth raked her bottom lip. "No buts. I have work to do still, and I can't be coming back over here for you later on."

"But Uncle Jax can bring me back."

"Uncle Jax has company."

Company she wouldn't even look at. She'd been doing a better job than normal of ignoring him. He couldn't decide if he should be grateful or disappointed.

"Just a few more minutes, Mom?"

"Listen to your mom, son." Jax's words brooked no argument. "I need some man time with Bren, so he's going to stick around."

That sounded more like an order than a request and it had Bren wondering what Jax wanted to talk to him about. Lauren's brother sounded serious.

She held out her hand and Kyle clearly knew not to push matters. "See you tomorrow, Uncle Jax." He tried to smile, but his disappointment was so acute he couldn't muster the effort. "You, too, Bren."

"You bet," he said, holding his palm up in the air. "Gonna work you harder tomorrow."

That brought out the kid's smile. He slapped his palm against Bren's. "Can't wait."

But Lauren? She walked away without a backward glance, the light from the pool catching her hair and turning the ends nearly blond. It was a beautiful night. The fog that hugged the nearby coastline had incited a breeze, one that tugged at the branches of the oak trees and disturbed the surface of the pool, which rippled in response. It might have been too cold if not for the outdoor pizza oven, which still emitted heat and cast a glow over the tables and chairs. They watched as the two disappeared around the side of the house. A long walk. Bren couldn't believe the size of the place, nor how humble and down-to-earth its owner was.

"You're doing a good job with Kyle."

He looked up, met the man's gaze. He had a feeling Jax Stone didn't hand out praise all that often, and so he appreciated the spark of approval in the man's brown eyes. "Thanks."

"But I warn you Lauren's not going to be much help when it comes to Kyle riding steers. She's hoping it'll all go away."

He nodded his agreement. "I doubt it will."

Jax stood, crossed to the island where he'd been making pizza and opened the door of a mini refrigerator. "Want one?" He held out a bottle of beer.

"No, thanks." He wiped his hands on the front of his jeans. He'd been so nervous around Lauren that his palms had been sweating. "I don't drink."

Jax nodded his approval. "Smart man."

"Town sheriff."

Jax smiled as he took a seat. "Even smarter." He bent again. "Soda? Bottled water?" he called from behind the mini refrigerator.

"Water sounds good."

Jax handed him a clear bottle. Heat from the oven wafted toward them, still smelling of basil and garlic, although they had long since consumed the pizza.

"So what makes you think Kyle won't give up?"

He reminded him of himself a long time ago, but he didn't say that. "I suppose it's the look in his eyes." He frowned as he tried to put into words what he was thinking. "He's not approaching it for the thrill of things. It's more that he's trying to figure it out. As if riding a steer is a puzzle that he's determined to understand. I've seen that look before on the faces of a couple NFR qualifiers that I helped coach when they were young."

"Really?"

Bren nodded. Jax set his beer down. "She's going to fight you the whole way."

Bren frowned again between sips of his water. "She's not putting up much of a fuss now. I mean, I can tell she doesn't like watching her son fall off, but what mom does?"

Jax shook his head. "She's in the 'it's just a phase' stage. When the steers get bigger and he wants to try riding a bull, that's when it'll hit the fan."

He supposed Jax was right. "She's going to hate me for helping him."

Jax's brown eyes were as sharp as the tip of a knife and Bren could tell he didn't flinch from the truth. He liked that about the man.

"Nah. She's not like that. She's tough. Been alone

for four years now, and before that…" He shook his head again.

"Before that?" he prompted because he had a feeling this was important. Still, the man took his time replying.

"It was tough for her. I tried to be there for her after Paul died, but I was running a business overseas and there wasn't much I could do."

Paul. The dead husband. "How'd he die?"

Another direct stare. "He worked for me."

What? He had no idea why he'd assumed the man was a white-collar worker who'd died from a drunk driver or something, but that's what he'd thought. And as the realization sunk in, something else clicked into place, too. The way she shrank back from him. The guarded look in her eyes. Her inability to hold his stare for longer than five seconds.

"They were having problems," he guessed.

Jax's head snapped up. His eyes narrowed. "How'd you guess that?"

"Just a hunch."

Jax took another long pull from his beer. "Paul Danners was an ass."

Bren had a feeling if Jax didn't like you, there was probably a good reason why. The man struck him as a straight arrow.

"If I had a customer I didn't like or who was difficult to deal with or had a huge ego, Paul Danners was my go-to guy. He'd pop off on the person and it either brought them into line or prompted a phone call, at which point I would explain that when it came to guarding precious assets, you don't want Mr. Nice Guy."

"But Mr. Mean Guy was married to your sister."

"He was, and God help me, a part of me hated him for what he put her through."

And that put him between a rock and a hard spot. "It must have been tough."

"It was harder on Lauren. I think she hid the worst of it from me."

Really bad, then. No wonder she was so protective of her son. And so closed off. He could almost sense the wall she had put up around herself.

"There's a part of me that wonders if I didn't send him on that last job on purpose."

Was that guilt he saw in the man's eyes?

"I knew sending him to Africa was dangerous."

"Africa?"

Jax nodded. "My firm works around the world. Somalia pirates. Nasty business. I knew it'd be dangerous."

He'd heard private contracting was a lucrative business, but clearly Jax had taken it to the highest levels.

"I still don't know how it happened. The government officials were less than helpful. All I know is he ended up dead on my watch."

"Were you there?"

Jax shook his head. "I don't get involved anymore. Not on that level."

"But you still own the business."

"Which makes it ultimately my fault."

And it tore him up. Even though he wasn't there. Even though he hated the way the man treated his sister. Even though the man was a jerk, it still ate at him.

"I guess I have Paul to thank for all this." He glanced around him. "It's because of him that I decided to slow down. Even though I'm not entirely certain what 'this' is just yet."

Trying to make amends somehow. That's what "this" was, but Bren kept that thought to himself, too.

"Anyway, Lauren has scars, and they run deep, especially where my nephew is concerned. She's hyper-protective. Sometimes overindulging, hence the steer riding even though she hates it, and independent to the point of stupidity. Kyle is the only reason why she moved to Via Del Caballo, despite that she needed the help in a bad way." He became lost in his thoughts for a moment and Bren wondered what it was that put such a sad look on his face. He watched as the man sucked in a breath and refocused on him. "I'm glad she's here, but I thought you might need a heads-up."

"About what?"

For the longest time Jax simply stared. Bren had a feeling he wanted to tell him something, but then he shrugged and said, "Eventually she might try to stop Kyle from riding."

A light flicked on nearby and he wondered if it was Lauren's room. Could she hear them? He doubted it. Jax didn't seem like the type to build flimsy walls, but it did something to him to know that she was there, maybe even stripping out of that sexy shirt…

No.

He wouldn't go there. If ever there was a good reason to steer clear from Lauren, Jax had just spelled it out. She came with baggage piled as high as a cruise ship. He'd be a fool to let her pretty face sucker him into thinking…

What, exactly?

He took a sip of his water, waiting, wondering what Jax had really wanted to say. Whatever it was, he'd changed his mind.

"She's had a tough go these past few years. I'm hoping she'll find happiness here, but I have a feeling her marriage to Paul will make that difficult. And I have a feeling her overprotective nature will make your life difficult."

Bren met Jax's gaze. There it was again. The look. He had a feeling there was a deeper message, but for the life of him he couldn't figure out what, and so all he said was "Thanks."

Chapter Seven

She didn't want to go.

"This is going to be so cool!"

Kyle did a little jump, arms lifting, heels all but clicking, the grin on his face as they headed into the Will Rogers Stadium as big as an orange slice.

"Can you believe it? All-access passes. I can't wait to meet Trent Anderson and Jim Conners and Dylan Anderson."

And she couldn't wait to come face-to-face with a man she wanted to see about as much as she wanted her teeth drilled into. He made her feel weak. As if she didn't have control of herself. After four years of keeping her guard up, she found it frightening to realize you couldn't control sexual attraction.

"You think I can get their autographs?"

"I'm sure you can."

"Cool."

They headed up some concrete steps. At the top level, parked in front of a row of double doors, were brand-new trucks, the logo of the series sponsor emblazoned on their sides, their chrome catching the last rays of the evening sun. Cowboys and cowgirls, most of them dressed in jeans and hats, walked along with them. She'd had no idea there were so many bull-riding fans in Southern California, but clearly they were all at tonight's performance.

"Tickets, please?" said a wiry-built young man who seemed thoroughly bored with his job.

"Right here," said Kyle, flashing a plastic card at the man.

The kid didn't seem impressed, just waved them through. Lauren looked around for Jax. He was supposed to meet them. She reached into her pocket, checked her cell phone. No message.

"Let's go find our seats." She tried to take Kyle's hand, but he stepped away from her and she shook her head. He'd been going through a phase, becoming more independent. It about broke her heart when he asked her not to kiss him out in front of his new school.

"We're up front right by the action." Kyle skipped ahead of her.

"Wait. How do you know what seats we're in?"

He flicked his pass. "It's written right here."

It was. She just hadn't expected him to figure that out. Maybe she did baby him too much, she thought, pausing at the top of a long row of steps that descended to an arena floor. Kyle was already halfway down. He kept looking down and she realized he was staring at the painted letters on the floor. Maybe she *should* give him some more freedom.

"Here it is," he called up to her. Goodness, they really were front and center. She wondered how the town sheriff had scored such amazing seats but then froze when she heard a voice behind her say, "Not bad, huh?"

She shivered because there it was again. The deep

timbre of his words. That's all it took. Just the sound of him to make her go all weak at the knees.

"It's amazing."

Deep breath. Paste a smile on your face. Turn and face him.

Dear God he was handsome. He stood on the main mezzanine, two steps above her, wearing another black shirt, the kind with a star embroidered onto the pocket. Staring down at her like he did, eyes dark and smoky, he reminded her of the old-time movie posters. Like one of those sexy older cowboys who appeared in 1950s movies.

"You should see behind the chutes."

She had to force herself to hold his amber-colored gaze. Beneath his black cowboy hat his eyes picked up the light from the arena roof, making them seem to sparkle. Or maybe that was amusement in his gaze, although what he found funny she had no idea. His black shirt had been tucked into jeans held up by a black belt that supported a buckle as big as her fist. She read the words Bull Riding before suddenly being aware that she stared at his crotch. She looked up quickly, her face flaming.

And now he looked on the verge of laughter.

She avoided his eyes, resolutely staring at the activity in the center of the stadium. Down below, a corner of the floor had been turned into a rodeo arena, complete with bright yellow fencing and cattle chutes along the back. It smelled like wet earth and livestock with just a hint of popcorn mixed in. None of the animals had been loaded yet, but cowboys crawled around the ironworks like monkeys on a tree. Colorful sponsor banners hung on the gates, the sheer scope of the equipment involved in producing the event mind-boggling.

"Come on. I think Kyle will bust a gut if we don't get behind the chutes soon."

He was probably right. Kyle waved his arms wildly when he spied who stood behind her. "I don't know where my brother is," she murmured, more to herself than him.

"He's not coming."

She stopped so suddenly he crashed into the back of her. He caught her around the arms. She turned to face him. He was already tall, but taller while standing on the step above her, and she hated the way her feminine side went all gooey, and the way his big hands felt around her upper arm, and how her whole body reacted to his nearness.

Good golly, Miss Molly.

"What do you mean, he's not coming?"

The smile in his eyes finally arrived on his face. "He called me earlier. Said something about getting hung up at a friend's place. Said he couldn't get ahold of you to tell you, so he called me."

Couldn't get ahold of her? What the heck was he talking about? She'd checked her phone at least a dozen times since they'd arrived. There weren't any messages.

"I wish he'd told me."

"Why?" His smiled faded. "Would you have changed your mind about coming tonight?"

Would she have? "That would have disappointed Kyle."

His eyes slid past her and landed on her son. "So let's not disappoint him."

He stepped toward her, his hand catching the crook of her elbow and gently turning her around. She stepped ahead of him, breaking the contact, but not because his touch made her fearful. Quite the opposite. She had to get away from him because she didn't trust herself not to overact in a way that would draw his attention, maybe even make him notice what she tried to hide from him.

"Can we go down and meet the bull riders?" Kyle pleaded.

Her son didn't waste any time, dancing on his toes and wiggling back and forth—like a puppy greeting his favorite human.

"Of course," Bren said.

"Now?" he asked, looking at her this time.

What could she say but, "I don't see why not."

Kyle's smile was something to behold. So wide and happy and pleased that it instantly made her forget her own troubles and tugged at her heart instead. It'd been so long since he'd looked at her like that. When Paul had died, she'd had to move to the poor side of town. She'd hated dropping him off at school, where he had no friends. He'd been miserable. She hadn't known exactly how miserable until they'd moved in January and he'd started his new school and she realized her little boy was back. The one who smiled when he woke up and didn't mind going to school in the morning. Just no kissing him goodbye.

"You coming?" Bren asked. She realized then that Kyle had scooted past her already. Bren waited for her to follow.

"How do we get down there?" she asked, more to cover her embarrassment than out of any real curiosity.

"Back doors. Secret stairwells. The usual."

He was playing with her, trying to tease her, which meant he'd picked up on her mood and how distracted she was. Great.

"Lead the way," she said, motioning him in front of her.

He hesitated. She waited because for some strange reason she didn't want him watching her walk up those steps.

"You don't always have to be in charge, you know."

The words rocked her back on her heels. "What?"

"You can just relax and let me take charge."

What was he saying?

"Your brother told me you work too hard and that you needed a break. I figure tonight you can do that. Relax. Enjoy yourself."

She would kill Jax. She glanced up the steps. Kyle waited for them at the top. He smiled. Waved. It took every ounce of willpower she possessed to smile back.

"Thanks." She took a step. "I'll try."

He grabbed her hand. She was so startled she turned back to face him, and this time she was level with him, and her eyes instantly found his lips.

"Do more than try."

She sucked in a quick breath, and he let her go. She gulped and spun around so fast her long hair flicked her in the face. She couldn't get out of there fast enough.

HE'D SCARED HER OFF.

Bren cursed himself inwardly for about the third time. He shouldn't have touched her. That had been a mistake.

Why a mistake?

He had to remind himself that he didn't want a relationship. That single life suited him just fine. That she looked about half his age in her tight jeans and beige shirt with rhinestones across the front. At least she'd left her hair down today, but that was almost as bad as when she had it in pigtails because the long brown strands framed her cheekbones and made her face look tiny and her eyes seem huge. Gorgeous didn't begin to describe her. And so if he scared her off, that was good.

Election year, remember? he reminded himself.

Kyle slammed through the door he'd led them to, Bren saying, "Easy there, partner," at the crashing sound the thing made.

"Sorry," the kid said, shooting him a look of contrition.

He liked her son. He liked the kid a lot. He was so full of boyish enthusiasm. So completely thrilled to be at the bull riding tonight. So happy about everything—from the corn dog vendor on the mezzanine floor to the souvenir booth right behind them.

"You need to calm down, Kyle," Lauren said, following in his wake. "You could have hurt someone bashing through the door like that."

The kid's eyes grew huge and Bren found himself patting him on his head. "It's okay. Just slow down, bud. We don't want you knocking over a bull rider, do we?"

That made him smile again. "No, sir."

And off he went, down the long concrete sidewalk that led to the arena floor. He leaped. He spun. He all but danced his way down and Bren couldn't help but smile.

"He's a good kid."

She nodded, but he could tell she was still tense, and he knew why. He wasn't an idiot. He'd seen the way her gaze had caught on his lips. Had watched as color spread beneath her skin. Knew she'd felt the same current of energy as he'd felt when they'd stood at eye level.

"He could barely sleep last night," she admitted.

That was better. At least they were conversing. "Did he ride yesterday?"

She nodded. "Jax helped him saddle up."

He smiled as he recalled the halter that first day. "Did they manage to get the saddle on right this time?"

There it was. The thing he'd been looking for. The thing he wanted to see even though there was no good reason why he should want her to smile. It was a little grin, but it would work. "They did."

The air turned cooler. He saw her shiver. "Cold?"

"No, I'm all right."

They'd reached the bottom floor, Kyle standing in front of a curtain that had an opening in the middle blocked by a security guard.

"This your kid?" the big burly man asked them.

"Yes," Lauren said warily.

"He tried to duck past me."

"Kyle!" she chastised.

"But I have a pass, Mom."

"You can't go in there alone," the man said.

If ever a kid looked crushed, Kyle Danners was the poster child. His shoulders sagged; his head bowed; his feet shuffled the dirt beneath his brand-new Western boots.

"It's okay," she told the security guard. "We've got him."

The man nodded and stepped back. Kyle instantly perked up. He took two steps beyond the curtain and stopped in his tracks. "Woooowwwwww!"

It was wow, all right. Ahead were green pipe panels that held a pen full of bulls bigger than any he'd seen in a long, long time. They stood there completely unbothered by their surroundings, surveying the crowd of people who walked between the main arena and the prepping area in the back of the coliseum. To the right, stock contractors and other officials made sure everything was as it should be. He turned left, knowing where he needed to go. There was a room in the back where everyone hung out until the performance started. That wouldn't be for another hour, but he'd texted Trent Anderson to make sure he'd arrived. Little did Kyle know that he was waiting for them in the back room.

"Slow down there," he warned Kyle.

Lauren caught up to her son, grabbing his hand. She shot him an apologetic look. He just smiled, motioning her to hold up. There was a door ahead, one that said No Admittance.

"You ready?" he asked Kyle.

The kid looked up at him, obviously confused. "For what?"

He went to the door and opened it. Inside, a half-dozen cowboys sat around on benches or on the floor or alongside the wall, each one performing his pre-show ritual, which might be reading or listening to music or rubbing rosin on his bull rope. That's what Trent Anderson was doing, his rope hanging from a wire on the wall, his face breaking into a huge smile beneath his black cowboy hat when he spotted them standing by the door.

"Well, as I live and breathe. Boys. Look who just walked in the door."

Eyes swiveled in his direction, a few he recognized, more he didn't, but those he did widened in surprise and then he was being crushed from behind in a giant bear hug by Trent, who'd crossed the room faster than a rooster after a hen. "Where have you been, boy?" he asked, spinning him around.

"Chasing bad guys," he answered.

Trent drew back, made scary fingers and said, "Ooooh. He has a gun."

Someone else clapped him on the back. One of the guys bashed the brim of his hat and Bren wondered why he'd stayed away so long. It'd been years since he'd been to a bull-riding event. Years since he'd watched his friends perform. Oh, he still tried to see Trent when he was in town or if he found himself up north, but he hadn't attended an actual performance in nearly a decade. It made him long for the old days.

"Come on. Let me introduce you to a few of the new guys," Trent said.

"Wait." He looked back to where Lauren and Kyle stood by the door. "First I'd like you to meet one of your biggest fans."

Trent's silver eyes followed his gaze, smiling when he caught sight of Kyle. But then he spotted Lauren, and Bren watched as he broke into a flirtatious grin, one that Bren knew was completely harmless because the bull rider had been happily married for years, and said, "Howdy, ma'am. Always happy to meet a fan." He completely ignored her son.

"No," Kyle cried. "Not her. Me."

Trent stopped, pasted a confused look on his face and looked down at Kyle. Bren couldn't have loved a man more than he did in that moment. He might be one of the most famous bull riders in the sport's history, but he'd never let it get to his head.

"You?" he teased. "Why, you don't look old enough to know what bull riding is."

Kyle's eyes were wide when he said, "I do, too." He drew himself up. "I'm ten, and I know you've won the average six times. I know you were in a horrible accident years ago. I know you've already qualified for the finals for this year."

Trent glanced over at him, wiggling his brows. "Kid's a regular record book."

"Like I said. Your biggest fan."

That started what must have been a dreamlike experience for the little man, one that Bren was only too happy to have a hand in providing. He'd never seen a kid so excited to meet bull riders. Not even some of his former students had been able to recite statistics like Kyle Danners did. By the time they were ready to leave, it was hard to say who was more impressed, Kyle or the bull riders he'd met.

"That was the coolest thing in the world." Kyle's grin was second only to that of a child who'd seen Santa Claus on Christmas morning. "I'll never forget that for as long as I live."

He said the words with such absolute reverence and conviction that Bren knew he wouldn't. He caught the look on Lauren's face, the way she smiled gently down at her son. How she touched his hair, lovingly, and he wondered what it would have been like if his own mother had been so gentle. But that was a road he didn't like to travel, and so he said, "Ready to watch them ride?"

"You betcha." Kyle shot off toward the grandstands. Lauren slowed her steps and Bren knew she wanted to say something.

"Thank you," she said when their gazes connected. "You have no idea how much this means to him."

He thought about when he was Kyle's age. How he would have killed to meet one of his heroes. "Oh, I think I do," he said, for some reason feeling the need to stuff his hands in his pockets.

You want to touch her.

He did, he admitted. He wanted to grab her hand again, to squeeze it, to let her know without words that he knew what it was like to be a ten-year-old kid crazy about riding bulls.

"Why'd you walk away from it?"

He glanced at Kyle. The boy was waiting for them, peeking their way in between staring up at a banner that hung on one of the pipe panel fences.

"Long story."

She held his gaze and he felt himself sink deeper. It made him dizzy, that feeling, and that's when Bren knew he wouldn't be able to fight it. Whatever this was between them, it went deeper than mere physical attraction. There was something in her eyes. Something that drew him to her. Something that made him want to ask her why she looked so sad from time to time.

"Well, I hope one day you'll tell me."

He had a feeling he would. She turned toward her son, waving. He hung back for half a heartbeat, scrubbing a hand over his face.

This was getting complicated.

She glanced back at him and there it was again. That soft smile. That warm gleam in her eyes. For once she didn't look up at him as if he were a possible threat. Her hair fell in soft waves around her shoulders as she turned back again.

Complicated, but quite possibly worth it.

Chapter Eight

"Mom! They're doing it again!"

Lauren pulled her gaze away from the action in the arena and glanced in the direction her son had pointed, even though she knew what he looked at. A Jumbotron hung in the middle of the coliseum, and Kyle kept hoping they'd put his image up on-screen.

"Which camera is it?" Bren asked, glancing around as he tried to match up the camera angle to the people waving on TV.

"I think that one." Kyle pointed. Bren leaned in and laughed with Kyle as they tried to get the attention of the cameraman.

He was good with kids. She had to look away because watching him with her son did funny things to her insides. Oh, heck. Just being with him did funny things to her insides.

The crowd erupted. Lauren sat at the edge of her seat as a bull shot out of the gate with its rider clinging to the back of the brindle-colored animal with all his might. Didn't do him any good. With a snort and a spin, the bull was clearly going to unseat the cowboy. Lauren watched, breathless, as he tried—and failed—to hang on. He looked like a man dumped from a plane, arms akimbo, legs spread, only he didn't have a parachute. She covered her eyes when he landed.

And this was what her son wanted to do. What he dreamed about doing. What the man next to her would teach him to do.

"It's okay."

She felt his warm hand on her jean-clad thigh and her whole body tensed in another way. She didn't want to open her eyes. She really didn't, but he lightly squeezed and she felt compelled to meet his gaze.

Dear goodness.

His gold eyes were full of reassuring compassion. "He's got years before he'll be riding at this level. Heck. He might never get to this level. He might forget all about bull riding once he discovers girls."

She gulped and looked down at the fingers on her leg. "Maybe," she muttered, then clasped her knees together and shifted away.

He withdrew his hand, and she breathed a sigh of relief.

"You don't look convinced."

She wasn't. There was just something about the way Kyle talked about growing up to become a cowboy. It wasn't little-boy fantasies, she didn't think. His feelings went deeper than that. Something in his eyes. It was there right now as he leaned forward and watched the bull in the arena. A fascination. A curiosity. But most important, a determination and a look of utter confidence. The bulls didn't scare him.

"I have a feeling he's in this for the long haul."

When she glanced up at him, she saw it in his eyes, too. He knew. He wasn't surprised by her answer. Not at all. He felt the same way.

"The good news is he's going about things the right way. He's learning. Not just jumping on any old thing that moves and hoping for the best. He's working at it."

"Yeah, but it doesn't matter how hard he works, does it?" She took a deep breath and said the words she'd been keeping to herself for weeks. "He's going to get hurt."

He nodded and she had to look away because just the thought of it scared her to death. That's when she felt it again. His hand. This time it landed on her own hand, gently clasping it, and she looked into his eyes and it was as if the seats they sat on suddenly shot up to the heavens and it was just the two of them. She watched as his gaze moved to her lips and everything inside her tensed because it was almost as if...

He liked her.

She pulled back again.

He *liked* her.

As in found her attractive.

"They're doing it again!"

The words jerked her back to earth. Her son pointed at the Jumbotron and a couple appeared on-screen, but only for a split second because a heart covered the screen, one that opened up to frame the couple's heads, *x*'s and *o*'s dancing around the edges.

"What are they doing that for?"

"It's the kissing cam," Bren explained. "They're supposed to kiss each other."

"Eeeewwwww," Kyle said.

The sound almost made her laugh, especially when the couple kissed. There was no mistaking Kyle's groan of disgust.

"I'm thinking it might be a while before you have to worry about him kissing girls," Bren said.

She nodded, not wanting to meet his gaze, worried about what she might see in it. "I think you're right."

The camera panned to another couple. In the arena someone else climbed aboard a big bull, one with horns the size of handlebars. They'd been chopped off at the ends, from what she could see between the bars of the bucking chute, but were no less intimidating.

"Why do they do that?" Kyle asked when the second couple kissed.

"It's a game." Bren leaned forward and smiled at her son. Once again her heart did that odd little flip. There was such kindness in his eyes. "If you don't do it, you'll get booed."

"But what if you don't want to kiss the girl?"

"Then you're in trouble," Bren provided.

The bull rider pulled on his rope, the long end of it held straight up in the air. Lauren tried to focus on the action in the arena, not what sitting next to Bren did to her heart. The crowd cheered and clapped because yet another couple on-screen had given each other pecks, this time on the cheek. Kyle wrinkled his nose, looking as grumpy as a ninety-year-old man.

And then they were on-screen, she and Bren, and at first she couldn't quite believe her eyes.

"It's you!" Kyle was once again her little boy, evidently forgetting his disgust with the kissing game, because he bounced up and down in his seat, eyes bright with excitement.

The heart appeared. Lauren looked up at Bren, her eyes clearly telling him, *No*.

Why he ignored the silent message she had no idea,

but she knew he was going to. There was heat in his eyes, and this time when his gaze landed on her lips, her entire body stiffened.

"Don't you dare," she warned.

"Oh, I dare," he answered back.

And then he kissed her. Not harshly or even quickly, but slowly and softly and oh so sweetly that it reminded her of what it was like to be cherished and loved and cared for by a man.

She wanted to cry.

It was the kindest, most gentle of kisses and she could smell him and taste him and she wanted more. Damn it. She wanted more.

Bren increased the pressure and for just a moment she wondered what would happen if she opened her mouth, if she let him kiss her like she wanted to be kissed because, yes, damn it, she liked how he made her feel. Wanted to do something crazy and out of control…with him.

He pulled back. She stared up at him in shock. He had the same stunned expression on his face.

"You kissed my mom."

Lauren's gaze shot to Kyle. He stared at them both in horror, but then a funny thing happened to the dismay in his eyes. The horror turned to fascination and then to acceptance and then even to delight.

"You like my mom," he announced, his frown turning to a smile as he leaned back, crossed his arms behind his head and turned his attention back to bull riding. "Cool."

SHE BARELY LOOKED at him the rest of the night.

He shouldn't have been surprised. He should have

been relieved. A momentary lapse of judgment. A toe dipped in a pool. He'd discovered the water was hot.

He wanted to dive in.

The crowd cheered. The cowboy down below in the arena stuck to his bull like a flea on a dog. He watched, barely paying attention as the clock ticked. Two seconds. Three seconds. He shouldn't have kissed her. Four seconds. But he didn't regret it. Five seconds. Six seconds. The last thought worried him the most. Eight seconds.

Kyle jumped up.

It was only as he caught a glimpse of the look on Kyle's face that he realized who it was that rode. Trent.

"He did it!" Kyle cried.

Yes. His friend had done it. And so had he, but he didn't care. That was the most shocking thing of all. He didn't care that tongues would wag and people would gawk if he dated someone at least ten years younger than himself. He liked her. And there was something there, something he couldn't explain and that he wanted to explore. If the people of Via Del Caballo were that small-minded, maybe it was time he moved on.

"Can we go down and see him?"

He glanced at Lauren, but she still wouldn't look at him. He would have to do something about that. She'd been working so hard lately. He doubted she'd had a break. He'd like to remind her that there was more to life than getting good grades and working your fingers to the bone.

"Sure, why not." Kyle fist-pumped the air.

They had to wait for one more competitor, but it was a short ride. Trent was the only one to cover his bull, and Bren couldn't help but beam with pride. There'd been a time when they weren't even sure Trent would ride again. If it hadn't been for Saedra, a barrel-racing friend from his rodeo days, forcing him into therapy, who knew what might have happened. That's where he'd met Alana, his wife. And now look. Two kids and winning again.

"Ready?" He stood. So did everyone else around them, Kyle rushing into the aisle.

"Kyle!"

The kid paused, shoulder slumping. Lauren got bumped by someone in the crowd and, automatically, his hands landed on her waist to steady her. He felt her tense, but he didn't let her go. She was warm to the touch and he caught a whiff of her—orange blossoms— and it was all he could do not to pull her up against him because she smelled so damn good.

"Come on. Come on." Kyle did a little jig. "We're going to miss seeing him."

"No, we won't." He watched as Lauren rushed forward to catch Kyle's hands. Clearly didn't want to be near him. Just as clearly, he knew she felt the same connection he did. She just didn't want to admit it.

They made it to the main foyer, Kyle sticking close to his mom as they retraced their steps. Their passes would get them to the arena floor and Kyle could barely contain his excitement when he realized he'd get to stand on the edge of the winner's circle and watch Trent get his prize check. It was all Lauren could do to keep him from bolting through the security checkpoint. Somehow he managed to wedge his way through the crowd, dragging his mom along, until he stood at the perimeter, halting only when he was right in front.

"Well, looks who's here."

He almost didn't recognize the voice, nor the dark-haired woman who stared up at him. The blue eyes, though, he recognized those. Alana Anderson. Trent's wife. He hadn't seen her since the birth of her first child, but she hadn't changed at all in the years he'd known her.

"Alana." He pulled her to him and hugged her, drawing back with a smile. "I was wondering where you've been hiding."

Her grin was so big it rivaled the one on her husband's face. "And I was wondering where you ran off to. Trent said he saw you earlier."

"He did. I had to introduce him to a friend."

Her gaze ducked past him, searching for that guest, no doubt. Her smile widened when she spotted Lauren. "Is that her? Is that your girlfriend?"

Bren drew back. So did Lauren, who was quick to shout over the din of the crowd, "I'm not his girlfriend."

"She's just a friend," he quickly said to assuage her embarrassment. "And this is her son." He motioned Kyle forward. "The future bull rider."

Alana bent down so she could shake Kyle's hand. "Nice to meet you, young man. Trent tells me you're riding steers right now."

"I am." Kyle glanced up at her proudly. "I'm too young to ride bulls."

"Don't sound so disappointed." She laughed a little, meeting Lauren's gaze. "I'm sure you'll be riding bulls soon enough."

The two women exchanged glances and it wasn't hard to understand what they said to each other so silently. Alana had just had her and Trent's second child. A boy they'd named Justin after a mutual friend who'd died in the accident that had injured Trent. In this day and age of father-son rodeo performers, there was a good chance Justin would ride some day, and so she had to be feeling some of the same concerns that Lauren did. Bren could see it in her eyes.

"I have a competition next weekend." Kyle's eyes were as bright as the light above the arena. "You should come watch."

"Kyle," Lauren laughed, pulling her son up against the front of her legs. "I'm sure Mr. and Mrs. Anderson have better things to do than drive two hours to Norco."

"Actually, we were spending some time touring Southern California." She smiled at him again, her dark hair coiling over one shoulder. "It's so rare that we get away from the kids these days, we thought we'd spend a few days at the coast before Trent's next performance in Las Vegas."

"Does that mean you'll come?"

Kyle looked like he'd died and gone to heaven. It made Bren's heart swell with something—what, he couldn't quite say. The kids was so obviously a fan of Trent's, and a fan of the sport, it filled him with as much pride as if he were his own kid.

"We might. Let's ask Trent."

They all glanced in the man's direction. He was just wrapping up his interview, one of those huge checks in front of him, and Bren whistled when he glimpsed the amount. Good payday. His friend's eyes caught on his wife and he smiled and motioned her forward. They hugged and exchanged a big kiss while cameras flashed and in their eyes Bren saw something so precious and rare that it made him doubt his long-held belief that love was just for fairy tales. It was why he'd been single for so long. Why he planned to stay single. Not everyone could have what Trent had.

"Kyle, come on over," Trent called.

Kyle's fantasy day reached a whole new level. With Lauren watching, her son took picture after picture in the winner's circle. Bren vowed to do something special for his friends because he honestly didn't think they could be more kind to the little boy.

"Mom!" Kyle ran over to them once the crowd started breaking up. "Trent said he'd come to my rodeo next week. He said after the rodeo we can all drive to Bren's place afterward and do dinner."

"Dinner? Afterward?" Clearly Lauren didn't know what to say. Just as clearly she didn't want to disappoint her son. "I mean…that's a lot of driving."

"Actually, we'll be in that area anyway. And we were planning on heading back to Bren's place. It's been a long time since we've spent some time with him," Alana said.

"Yeah, but I'm sure you're busy," Lauren said.

Trent came up to them. "Never too busy to see a friend. And it's been forever since I've watched a junior bull riding." He glanced at Bren. "Why not make a whole weekend out of it?"

"Steer riding," Lauren quickly corrected.

"For now," Trent said with a smile.

Bren watched as Lauren looked down at her son. He wanted to go to her then for some reason. To reassure her. Instead he said, "It'll be fun."

She pulled herself together quickly. "Well, I—"

"So it's a plan," Alana said. "Rodeo and then dinner afterward."

She wanted to wiggle out of it, but it hit him then that

he didn't want her to. That he wanted to spend more time with her and maybe see if that kiss they'd shared was just a fluke.

"I'll text you directions to the rodeo grounds." Bren took the decision out of her hands.

"Cool!" Kyle cried.

Chapter Nine

Kyle fell asleep the moment he tipped his seat back, which was just fine with Lauren because it gave her time to reflect.

That kiss...

Okay, so she didn't want to reflect too deeply on that. She'd rather focus instead on Kyle and how happy he'd been—the happiest she'd seen him in years. He'd told her just before they'd climbed in her car that this was the best night of his life. She had no doubt that it probably was, and she had Bren to thank for it.

It was just after ten and once she took the exit to Via Del Caballo, it was darker than an empty closet beyond her headlights. That was one of the things she'd had to get used to living way out in the country. No more streetlamps. Just the moon and stars and the occasional porch light off in the distance.

Her brother's place, though, that was lit up like a Christmas tree. He had a thing about lights. Always insisted he could see the perimeter of his property. Military thing, she surmised. She could see it from the road, although it was nearly a mile to the actual home. She crossed between two iron posts, stopping beneath a sign suspended across them that said DHR. She could never remember the gate code, had to look it up on her phone—it would drive her security-conscious brother crazy if he knew she had it stored there. Off to her left she could make out Reynolds Ranch. The Reynoldses had been the original owners of the land.

"We home?" said her sleepy little boy when she drove forward again.

"Almost."

Kyle didn't answer. Sensory overload, she thought with a smile. He'd be talking about this trip for days, probably weeks and months. Her smile faded. And she'd be thinking about it for weeks and months, too. Thinking about that kiss.

Nope. Don't go there.

Bull riding. She firmly changed the subject in her mind. Why did it have to be bull riding? She didn't think she'd survive him riding steers. Pray to the Lord he got tired of it before he graduated to the real deal. She pulled to a stop in front of her place and then as quietly as she could climbed out.

"Did you have fun?"

She about jumped out of her boots. Her brother parted from the shadows like the Invisible Man.

"How do you do that?"

She saw his shadow shrug. "Training."

"It's kind of creepy."

"It's who I am."

And it had been Paul, too. That required another change of subject. "Kyle had a great time." But then she frowned. "Although it would have been better if you'd been there. What happened to you? Bren said something came up?"

"Work," he said softly. "Always work."

She could see his face thanks to ambient light spilling toward them from the porch. She could tell by looking at his face that it was another one of those nights. Restless. Anxious. Exhausted. Her brother suffered from post-traumatic stress disorder. She'd realized it once she'd moved in last month. It'd provided an important clue as to why he'd built his home so far off the beaten path and why he'd built a multimillion-dollar ranch. He was looking for peace as much as the people he hoped to help.

"I thought you were taking it easy these days."

"That's what I thought, too."

Supposedly he'd turned over control of Darkhorse Tactical Solutions to his second-in-command, but not that she could see. Between building the house and working from home, he never seemed to get much rest. Particularly at night, ostensibly because a lot of his business was overseas, which required middle-of-the-night phone calls.

"Need some help?" he asked, having spotted Kyle asleep inside the car.

"Sure. You can grab him while I open the front door."

She was worried about her brother, especially after he'd bailed tonight. Something was up. She'd barely seen him over the last dozen or so years, not even at company parties when Paul had worked for him, but the more time she spent with him, the more she could tell something was wrong, something that not even spending two million dollars on a new ranch could cure.

"Come on here," he gently told Kyle as he pulled him into his arms.

"'Cle Jax," Kyle slurred, his little arms wrapping around his uncle's neck. Jax hadn't been around a whole lot while Kyle had been growing up, but they'd made up for lost time in the past few weeks. Her son adored her brother, and he should. She had a feeling Jax had built the ranch not just for himself, but for her son, too. He'd known how much Kyle had wanted to learn how to ride. How he'd dreamed of becoming a cowboy. And look. Here they were.

"Go on and get his bed ready," he told her.

She raced ahead, leaving the front door open. As she pulled back Kyle's covers, she had to admit, it was wonderful to have some help. To know that she had a roof over head—no matter what—and that her brother didn't mind her being there at all. It wasn't until that exact moment that it truly sank in—she wasn't alone any longer.

An image of Bren laughing with Kyle popped into her head.

No. He wasn't a part of the picture. Her brother was here to help, although why the realization hit her on this night, she had no idea, but suddenly she was so incredibly grateful she wanted to cry.

"I got this," she said to Jax when he entered the bedroom, not looking him in the eyes for fear he'd see her tears. She pulled off Kyle's boots, shooting him a small smile as he moaned in his sleep. He smiled, too, and she knew it was a happy smile. She made quick work of getting Kyle ready for bed. Her kid hardly batted an eye, just rolled over. She tugged the covers up over his shoulder, gave him a kiss, a love so pure and deep flooding her soul she could barely breathe for a moment.

"Did he get to meet Trent Anderson?" Jax asked the moment she came out into the hall.

She closed the door softly behind her. "Trent and a score of other bull riders whose names I can't remember."

"And how about you? Meet any celebrities that got you all excited?"

She shook her head as she walked toward the main living area. "I just sat back and watched."

And had her heart stopped when she'd been kissed. *No*, she told herself yet again. *Stop thinking about it. Now. It was just a game. A dare. It didn't mean a thing.*

Yeah, but it made you feel something.

She shook her head and focused on what she had to do before bed. The kitchen had a bar-level counter that separated it from the family room and Jax took a seat on one of the spinning stools. She poured herself some iced tea even though caffeine was the last thing she needed at this time of night.

"Want some?"

He shook his head. "You need to have more fun."

"Speaking of that, I'm going to have dinner at Bren's house next week."

Her brother's dark brows shot to his hairline. "Really."

"Stop." She shook her head. "It's not like that."

"No?"

"Kyle invited Trent Anderson to come watch him ride next week and one thing led to another and we're all having dinner after the Norco Junior Rodeo. You should come."

She saw his mouth tighten. "Maybe to the rodeo, but not promising dinner."

She should have figured as much. "Try. You could use a break."

"And you could use a night out on the town."

She about choked on a swallow of tea. "Excuse me?"

"I'm serious. You've been here, what? Six weeks? All I've ever seen you do is study and look for work."

Yeah, and the job search wasn't going so well. Employers wanted full-time employees. Not older college students with nearly a year left of school and a kid back at home.

"I just want to get done with school as soon as possible."

"You're not going to speed it up any. Slow down a little and enjoy yourself."

With someone like Bren. He didn't say the words, but she knew he was thinking them. First time her brother had tried to play matchmaker, but she was pretty sure that's what he was doing now.

"I'm not interested in dating anyone right now."

"I like him. From all I heard, he's a good man."

She nodded after taking another swallow. "He's got good friends, I'll say that much for him. Trent Anderson was the nicest guy I've ever met. His wife was sweet, too."

"So. Go out on a date with him. Valentine's Day is coming up."

She set her finished glass down by the sink. "I'm not dating anyone, big bro." She went up to him and kissed his cheek. "But thanks for thinking of me." She turned him toward the door. "Now leave me alone. I have a paper I need to finish."

"And you say *I* always work."

"Must run in the family."

He took the hint, though, and when the door closed, she rested her head against it. Valentine's Day. Hah. She didn't need to be wined and dined by anyone. She was fine all on her own.

Oh, yeah? asked a little voice.

Yeah, she told that voice back. And she almost believed herself.

IT WAS DAYS like the one that dawned that next Saturday that gave Southern California such a great reputation when it came to weather—clear and sunny and just a touch cool, which meant that by this afternoon it'd be the perfect temperature. The only fly in her ointment? Having to watch Kyle ride...and other things.

"You ready?"

Jax would be driving them all to the rodeo. That was probably a good thing since it was a couple hours away. Lauren didn't like the thought of having to pull over so she could throw up. Much easier just to carry a bag in her purse and let someone else do the driving.

"As I'll ever be."

For some reason she was more nervous today than the first time Kyle had climbed aboard a steer. It must have been the professional bull riders she'd watched. There'd been more than a few close calls that night...

Including your kiss.

...and it'd meant coming face to face with the dangers of riding a wild animal for "fun."

Fun. More like insanity.

"Let's go!"

Kyle was his usual exuberant self. Today he wore a cowboy hat that looked five sizes too big but that he'd refused to take off ever since Bren had given it to him. He'd had two lessons this week. One on horseback and one with the other kids. She hadn't been there for either. She'd had classes both days, and so Jax had taken over. She'd hated to miss Kyle's lesson, but on the other hand, it'd been great to steer clear of Bren. Being near him was just too damn disturbing.

You won't be able to avoid him today, taunted the little voice in her head that she'd begun to hate.

No. She wouldn't. But she'd have her brother and Kyle there. And Trent and Alana. And the Reynoldses, she'd been told by Kyle. They were their neighbors to the south and mutual friends of her brother and Bren.

They all piled into Jax's brand new F-350—a truck that Lauren planned to buy for herself...one day. If she didn't get distracted from her studies. Or let a man get in the way of her goals.

"I wonder if the steer will be big today."

Lauren's stomach tumbled end over end. She didn't want to think about that.

"Bren said it doesn't matter what size the steers are. What matters is the size of my heart."

Hopefully no wild animal would step on that heart. And hurt her baby. And destroy her life, because she didn't want to think about a world without Kyle in it.

Dear Lord, how would she get through this day?

Jax seemed to sense her anxiety. He shot her a reassuring grin and she wondered why it was the men in her life craved adventure so much. Was that where Kyle got it from? Had Paul passed on his love of an adrenaline rush?

"He'll be fine, Lolo."

Her gaze jerked to his own. Lolo. She hadn't heard the nickname in years. Before he'd rushed off to join the military, he'd called her that all the time. And then he'd left her and things had never been the same.

"I'm counting on it," she answered softly.

The rodeo grounds looked as crowded as a truck

stop. One of the things that always surprised her was the number of expensive horse trailers on the grounds. The professional cowboys had nothing on their junior competition, or at least the parents of the steer wrestlers and ropers and barrel racers. Thank goodness Kyle didn't want to do that. She'd never be able to afford a trailer on her own.

"I'll go get my number."

"Kyle—" But her son was already jumping out of the truck.

"Let him go," Jax said, watching him run away, the door of the truck still open. "He'll be fine."

He would be. She'd learned rodeo was like a huge family. Bren seemed to know everyone in the industry and Kyle said he'd introduced him to a bunch of people. She knew he'd be okay. It was just strange to have him run off and do stuff without her.

Better get used to that.

In this case, she knew the little voice was right. Eight more years was all she'd have him for, because she knew her son wouldn't be the type to live at home forever. He had too many things he wanted to do in life, and the determination and focus to do them.

"You ready for this?"

The voice was Bren's and she didn't need to turn around to know that he would be every bit as disturbing in the flesh as he had been in her dreams.

"I don't think she's ever going to be ready."

Jax came around the front of his truck, hand outstretched. Bren shook it and clapped him on the back in the way that men did. She didn't want to notice how handsome Bren looked in his pressed blue jeans and white button-down shirt topped off by a black hat.

When their gazes connected, his eyes sparked in the same way as her body did when she felt that gaze meet her own.

She was kidding herself.

All week long she'd told herself that the spark she felt was just her imagination. That the brief kiss they'd shared was nothing more than the kiss of strangers. Now she knew how badly she'd lied to herself.

"Hello."

It was all she could think of to say, all her sluggish mind could come up with because, gosh darn it all, she'd become completely tongue-tied.

"You okay?" he asked, concern in his kind eyes.

"She's trying not to hyperventilate," her brother said.

That was so close to the truth that she had to look away. "Just stressed out."

"Where's Kyle?"

"Off getting his number," Jax answered for her. "Ran off like a bat out of hell the moment we parked."

"He probably can't wait to see who he's drawn."

She hadn't even thought about that, but Bren was probably right. Kyle had spent hours on the internet this week looking up which steers had gotten what score on what day. She'd had no idea such stats were online, but Bren must have told him about them. He'd been hoping all week for a steer named Exterminator, an animal known for its wild bucking and crazy spins. Lauren had prayed all week he'd get a different steer, perhaps one named Easy Rider.

"I'm kind of curious, too," Bren admitted. "Let's go see."

"What about Alana and Trent?" she asked. "Are they meeting us here?"

"They're on their way. I told them to call me when they got here."

They all followed Bren toward the announcer's stand. A few people nodded at Bren when they caught sight of him walking with her. One of the old cowboys even tipped his hat and said, "Sheriff," the gesture so old-fashioned it might have made her smile if she weren't so on edge. Clearly the old guy was someone who lived in Via Del Caballo and knew who he was.

The Norco rodeo grounds were surrounded by barren hills dotted with shrubs and oaks. Trucks and trailers were scattered here and there, all of them vying for coveted shade. Metal pipe panels served as the bucking chutes, the arena made of the same metal bars. The smell of animals—horses and steers and sheep—filled the air. There'd be mutton busting first, she'd been told, tiny little kids clinging to the backs of shaved animals. Kyle wouldn't ride until the very end, which meant she had at least two hours of anxiety attacks ahead of her.

"I got him! I got him!"

Kyle ran up to them, face red from either exertion or excitement, because she didn't need to know who he meant by *him*.

Damn.

"You got Exterminator?" Bren asked.

"I sure did."

He looked almost as proud as if he'd already ridden the darn thing.

"Good for you."

Let's hope it was good for him, said The Voice, *because it would really suck to make a trip to the hospital on such a nice day.*

"I'm going to run back to the truck and get my stuff."

Because it made perfect sense to prepare equipment hours before the need for it, but she understood his reasons. Bren had explained it was the routine. Rubbing rosin on a bull rope was like someone meditating before a ride. It gave a person time to prepare the mind. Bren, the Zen Master.

"You want to go find seats?" Jax glanced toward the grandstands. "Might want to grab some shade while we can."

"Sure," Bren said.

Lauren looked in Kyle's direction. She wanted to follow him. To see if he needed help.

To hover.

It was the hardest thing she'd had to master in recent weeks—the ability to let her kid go. She couldn't change who he was, but she could change the way she thought. At least today she wasn't thinking about Bren's kiss every five seconds. That was a plus.

"You okay?" said the man in question.

"Fine."

Jax had walked off. She saw him glance back, but rather than wait for them, he kept on going. Traitor.

"You don't look fine."

She lifted her chin. "I'm just tired." No sleep the night before a rodeo would do that to a person.

He took a step toward her. She had to tell herself not to move.

"Try not to stress."

She almost laughed. "Is that what you used to tell yourself?"

He took another step. They were inches away now, so close she could feel him next to her, his presence like an invisible force field that she could sense.

"It's what I tell myself every day." He had a dimple. Just on the left side of his mouth. It came into play when he smiled. "Believe me. These days it's more dangerous to do my job than it is to climb on a bull."

Yes, she admitted, inhaling the tangy scent that was him. It was dangerous. Yet he did it. Just like Paul had gone out and done his job. But he was not like Paul, because she could never remember her husband staring down at her in the way that Bren did now.

"He'll be okay," he said softly and then, horrors upon horrors, he cupped the sides of her face, caressing her cheeks lightly with the soft pads of his thumbs, his face lowering, and she thought he would kiss her. Goodness, she admitted to herself that she *hoped* he would kiss her, because she needed his comforting touch and the sweetness in his eyes like she needed air to breathe and food to survive. "I promise."

And then he let her go and she felt like a balloon whose strings had been cut; she wanted to take flight or maybe sink to the ground.

He turned and followed her brother, leaving her there. Alone.

"Oh, my."

It was all she could think to say.

Chapter Ten

He'd almost kissed her.

There in front of God and what felt like half the citizens of Norco.

So? he told himself. He was a grown man. What did it matter if he dated someone younger than he was? Who would care? Well, aside from a few locals who'd made the trek to Norco.

"I'm glad you're here," Jax said as they took their seats on aluminum bleachers. "You can teach me about what these kids are doing." And then his gaze slid past him and he must have realized his sister hadn't followed. "Where's Lauren?"

"I think she went to help Kyle."

He'd spooked her. He'd seen it in her eyes.

"She's not taking this whole steer-riding thing well."

They'd talked during Kyle's lessons. He liked Lauren's brother. A lot. They were cut from the same cloth. They both cared about community and service and helping others, and he had a feeling whatever happened, they would end up good friends.

"It just takes time," Bren said, trying to spot her back behind the rodeo chutes. He'd seen her heading back toward Kyle, had known she needed to collect herself, and so he'd let her go.

"You mind me asking something?"

Bren tipped his hat back a bit as he turned toward Lauren's brother. "What?"

"Why the hell haven't you asked her out?"

He rocked back. "Excuse me?"

"Kyle told me you kissed her."

Okay, so that was a line of questioning he didn't expect. "Just at the bull riding. It was one of those kissing cams."

"My nephew said it lasted longer than everyone else."

He glanced down at his boots. At his hands. At his lap. Why did he suddenly feel about seven years old? He couldn't even tell the man it had been a mistake, because it hadn't been one. He'd been thinking about that kiss all week.

"So what is it?"

He took a deep breath. "She's too young for me."

Jax's eyes widened for just a moment before he smiled and shook his head. "No, she's not."

He met the man's gaze. "I'm an elected official. And even though she's twelve years younger, she looks about twenty years younger, and I could just see the raised eyebrows—"

"So what?"

"The last thing I need is a bunch of tongues wagging."

"I could see that being a concern, yes, but you like her," he pronounced. "She likes you. Take her on a date."

It sounded like more of an order than a suggestion. His eyes focused on one of the rodeo officials out in the arena. He appeared to be checking the ground and for a moment he wished he was back to riding bulls again. Life had seemed so much simpler back then.

Should he do it? Should he take the plunge? In their small, ultraconservative town, some people wouldn't like it. But maybe Jax was right. Maybe there was something else holding him back. He'd never let anything get in the way of something he wanted before.

"Take her on a date."

"She's having dinner with me tonight."

"She's going to a barbecue at your place. Not the same thing. Ask her out. On a proper date. Then see what happens."

He stared at the man. "You mind telling me why you want me to date your sister so much?"

Jax's eyes flicked to the action in the arena. It looked like they were about to start the rodeo, and judging by the number of people beginning to line up by the ingate, every kid in Norco must have been there to ride.

"I want her happy," he said simply.

He couldn't argue with that.

"HE'S HERE," KYLE SAID, the excitement in his voice on level with someone who'd just won the lottery. "I see him. Right there."

Kyle pointed toward the edge of the parking area and sure enough, in walked Trent Anderson and his wife, Alana.

"I'm going to go to them."

"Kyle," she called after him. "Just wait."

But he was off.

"You've been hiding from me."

She resisted the urge to duck behind the big rig she'd

been standing next to—a cattle truck—one with aluminum sides that reflected the sun into her eyes.

"I thought I would stay here." She grabbed her hair and pulled it over one shoulder, wishing for about the tenth time she'd braided it and put it into pigtails. It was hot standing by that truck. "In case Kyle needed me."

"I thought you'd want to sit up in the grandstands with us."

"I do." She forced a smile. "When it's Kyle's turn to ride, I duly promise to join you and my brother up there." She glanced after Kyle. "Don't you want to greet your friend?"

"And steal Kyle's thunder?" He had followed her glance, smiling at the sight of Kyle waving his arms frantically toward one of his new friends. It was clear Trent was recognized instantly because the kid's mouth dropped open and then he rushed forward. Soon Trent had a crowd around him, Alana looking beyond the excited faces and catching them staring at her. She smiled and waved.

"I should go over there," she said.

"Wait." Bren caught her by the hand.

"What." She stared at their hands.

"Your brother thinks I should take you out."

"Excuse me?"

He scrubbed a hand over his face. "Do you want to maybe go out? On a date. You know. Dinner. Maybe a movie."

A date? When was the last time… Had she ever been asked out on a…

"Do you?" he asked.

Alana walked toward her. Kyle and Trent still held

YOUR PARTICIPATION IS REQUESTED!

Dear Reader,

Since you are a lover of our books – we would like to get to know you!

Inside you will find a short Reader's Survey. Sharing your answers with us will help our editorial staff understand who you are and what activities you enjoy.

To thank you for your participation, we would like to send you 2 books and 2 gifts – **ABSOLUTELY FREE!**

Enjoy your gifts with our appreciation,

Pam Powers

SEE INSIDE FOR READER'S SURVEY

For Your Reading Pleasure...

We'll send you 2 books and 2 gifts
ABSOLUTELY FREE
just for completing our Reader's Survey!

YOUR READER'S SURVEY
"THANK YOU" FREE GIFTS INCLUDE:
▶ 2 FREE books
▶ 2 lovely surprise gifts

PLEASE FILL IN THE CIRCLES COMPLETELY TO RESPOND

1) What type of fiction books do you enjoy reading? (Check all that apply)
○ Suspense/Thrillers ○ Action/Adventure ○ Modern-day Romances
○ Historical Romance ○ Humor ○ Paranormal Romance

2) What attracted you most to the last fiction book you purchased on impulse?
○ The Title ○ The Cover ○ The Author ○ The Story

3) What is usually the greatest influencer when you <u>plan</u> to buy a book?
○ Advertising ○ Referral ○ Book Review

4) How often do you access the internet?
○ Daily ○ Weekly ○ Monthly ○ Rarely or never

5) How many NEW paperback fiction novels have you purchased in the past 3 months?
○ 0 - 2 ○ 3 - 6 ○ 7 or more

YES! I have completed the Reader's Survey. Please send me the 2 FREE books and 2 FREE gifts (gifts are worth about $10 retail) for which I qualify. I understand that I am under no obligation to purchase any books, as explained on the back of this card.

154/354 HDL GLNW

FIRST NAME · LAST NAME

ADDRESS

APT.# · CITY

STATE/PROV. · ZIP/POSTAL CODE

WR-217-SUR17

court. She used her new friend as an excuse to step back and say, "Can I get back to you on that?"

And she all but ran away. She'd just been asked out. *Asked out.*

"There you are," Alana said when the two met halfway between Bren and Trent. "I was just wondering if you were here."

A date.

"You okay?" Alana had goodness shining from her eyes and she couldn't help but respond.

"Not really." She peeked back to where Bren had been. He hadn't followed. He'd been waylaid by someone, the two deep in conversation, hands gesturing, his friend, an older man with a thick white mustache, listening intently. "I get a little stressed out when Kyle rides."

Alana's face cleared. "I know how you feel."

She would bet she did. She couldn't imagine being married to a man who rode fifteen-hundred-pound animals for a living.

"When I was pregnant, I swore I wouldn't watch Trent. Too much stress. I worried I might lose the baby."

She had no idea why the words took her by surprise, but they did. "Did you watch him, though?"

"Every ride." She turned so that she half faced her husband and Lauren admired how pretty she was with her dark hair loose down her shoulders and blue eyes sparkling. "When I married him, I knew what I was getting into. Sounds like you were kind of thrown into this whole deal."

"That's an understatement."

Alana smiled. "You're a good mom to be so supportive."

She snorted. "That's what everyone keeps telling me."

She laughed a little. "Well, Kyle's in good hands with Bren teaching him."

Yes. She had to admit that. The man was a saint when it came to dealing with her son. "How long have you known him?"

"Not as long as Trent." She glanced back at her husband. "Those two go way back. Bren helped Trent learn how to ride. When Bren quit, Trent kept going with it."

She felt her interest spike. "Why did he quit riding? Do you know? I've been wondering."

Alana frowned for a moment. "I do." She waited, hoping she'd share it with her. Alana studied her for briefly and whatever she saw must have reassured her. "It got away from him."

"What did?"

"This." She waved toward where Trent stood with the crowd of kids and now adults. "This whole thing. This crazy life."

It took her a moment to understand what she meant. "You mean he couldn't deal with fame?"

She turned to face her fully, her eyes suddenly serious. "In a way, I guess. Twenty years ago the sport was just going public. Bren was right on the cusp of it all. Television coverage. Big-time sponsors. Huge money. The girls were all crazy for Bren. It was a whole new world."

She glanced past Alana to Bren, still trying to comprehend. "He got cocky."

"No. Not according to my husband. It was the parties and the money and the lifestyle that got to him."

At last she finally understood.

"Trent was just starting out when Bren was—" she scrunched her brow as she thought about it for a moment "—early twenties, I guess. Anyway, Trent said Bren was like a rock star, drinking all the time, girls, fans, you name it. One night they were in Vegas celebrating some big win or something and Bren and a bunch of his buddies decided to ride some horses down Las Vegas Boulevard."

Bren? The town sheriff?

"Worst part is, the horses weren't theirs. They stole them from some riding stable near one of the casinos. Caused a big wreck. People went to the hospital. One of the horses almost died. Bad scene."

It was such a different image of Bren than what she had now. Unreal.

"Then next morning when he sobered up, Trent told me he quit. Just like that." She snapped her fingers. "He joined the Army, worked his way through the ranks, and when he got out, he settled here."

"Wow."

"You gotta respect a man that recognizes when something is bad for him, even if it's something he loves."

"Mom, Trent's going to help me get ready for steer riding."

She had to pull her thoughts back to the present to focus on her son and the man who stood behind him— Trent. Bren still hadn't followed and she wondered what he and the older gentleman were discussing so intently.

"That's great, honey."

She smiled a greeting at Trent, who'd gone up to his wife and planted a kiss on her cheek, and for a second she felt such a keen sense of longing it almost made her sick.

You gotta respect a man that recognizes when something is bad for him.

She'd been the opposite. She'd stuck it out with Paul even when his bouts of anger grew more obvious. She'd always shielded Kyle from it, and in some ways, that enabled the bad behavior. His insults had grown worse and worse and she'd just stood there and let him tear her down, let him convince her that she was stupid and incapable of doing anything with her life and impossible to love.

"You want to go up to the grandstands and watch?" Alana asked.

"Sure."

Alana led the way. Lauren glanced toward Bren, catching his eye, her heart quickening.

You're afraid he'll feel the same way about you. That he'll get to know you better and find out what a loser you are.

But she wasn't a loser. She'd proven to herself that she could work her way through school. That she could raise a son. That she could support herself. She wasn't stupid or useless or any of the other things Paul had called her. She deserved to be happy. Or at least have a shot at happiness. Heck, maybe she might even find someone to share her life with down the road, but that would happen only if she put her big-girl panties on and went out on a date with someone.

Someone like Bren.

Chapter Eleven

She was up there somewhere, Bren thought, scanning the grandstands in hopes of spotting Lauren. No doubt sitting on the edge of her seat.

"Brings back memories, eh?" Trent said, standing next to him. They stood over the wooden chutes and watched as the steer Kyle would ride in a just a few short minutes kicked the side in its eagerness to be released.

"It always does," he admitted.

Kyle stood next to him, the littlest steer rider, wearing the mandatory helmet on his head. He stared down at the animal he would climb aboard like a man would a mountain he planned to scale. It was such an adult look on such a little boy face that once again Bren found himself thinking he might just go all the way.

"Glad Alana convinced Lauren to sit with her up in the stands."

Yes, but she was probably digging her nails into her aluminum seat. Alana had all but dragged Lauren off, claiming she would only make her son more nervous by hovering, and so she'd left without a backward glance. He supposed that was her answer to his "go out with me on a date" question. Clearly she didn't feel the same way about him as he did about her.

It bummed him out.

That was the only way he could describe how he felt. She didn't want to go out with him. Like a high school kid who'd just been told his pick for prom was going with someone else, it had ruined his day.

"You ready to rock and roll?" Trent asked Kyle, interrupting the kid's near-trancelike stare.

All Kyle did was nod. That was the thing with him. He was a thinker. He didn't get all pumped up. Didn't jump around. Didn't act like a out-of-control idiot, all full of adrenaline. He tackled bull riding like he would a math problem.

"Okay, kids. Go ahead and get ready."

The rodeo official who spoke caught a glimpse of Trent standing there, his eyes widening for a moment before he came forward with his hand outstretched. It'd been like that all morning.

"Good to see you here, Mr. Anderson."

"Thanks," his friend said, helping Kyle over the rail while smiling at the man. Bren picked up the bull rope, dangling it over the side of the animal. Kyle helped guide it around while Trent used a wire rod to fish it out from beneath the steer's belly. It was a move they'd practiced and something that was important to get right. If you did it too fast, you might upset the animal. Everything had to be done gently and easily. The last thing they needed was the steer going crazy in the chute and potentially injuring Kyle.

"Got it?" Trent asked Kyle, who once again nodded.

There was fear on his face, Bren realized. But there was determination, too. He had the single-eyed focus of a military sniper.

"Sit down slow and easy," he told Kyle.

The kid did as he was told, pulling his bull rope as he went along. The steer danced around beneath him, but Kyle remained poised over his back, his feet standing on the bottom board of the chutes. He would be one of the first to go out. Bren glanced around and determined that the kid before him was settled all the way down on the steer's back.

"Looks like we've got our first contestant ready to ride!" the announcer said from above them. "This is Tate Briker from nearby San Luis Obispo."

The chute door opened and out jumped a steer. The poor kid never stood a chance. Half a jump and he was already off.

"Ready?" Trent asked.

Kyle nodded, sitting all the way down on the steer. He pulled his rope tight, wrapping it around his hand just as Bren had shown him. Not too tight. Not too loose. Above them the announcer asked the crowd to cheer for the fallen rider. It would take a moment to get the steer out of the arena, and with each second that passed, Bren's heart rate increased. He knew Lauren had to be suffering up in the stands. He wished he were next to her, but she would only rebuff his attention.

The rodeo staff closed the gate on the previous steer, and Bren slapped Kyle on top of the helmet.

"Ride hard."

Quick nod this time, and it was all the latch man needed to see. The gate swung wide. Kyle's body rocked backward as the steer reared up, but damned if he didn't stick with it.

"Hang on!" Trent yelled.

One jump, and then two; Kyle hung with the steer each time. All the hard work, all the time spent in the saddle, it paid off. The difference in his riding this week from last was night and day, and Bren felt his chest swell with pride.

"That's it," he heard himself say.

At this rate the boy might cover.

The steer spun right. Kyle almost lost it. But with strength and a healthy dose of grim tenacity he stayed on. Three jumps, four. Any second now the horn would blow. The steer turned right. Then right again. And again. Kyle leaned into the well, the fringe on his chaps sticking straight out, and Bren's heart stopped for a few seconds, but then the horn sounded and he let out a yell that must have deafened Trent.

Kyle couldn't get off.

Not safely. Bren's excitement faded as he realized the predicament the kid was in. The steer still turned in circles, centrifugal force keeping Kyle toward the middle. He let go of the bull rope, thrust himself to the left. The rear of the steer caught him as he tried to fling himself off, launching Kyle ten feet in the air.

"Kyle!" he cried, already on the move before the boy landed. He nearly fell to his knees when his boots hit arena dirt. The steer ran off. Kyle hadn't moved.

"Kyle!" he yelled again. He reached him at the same time the rodeo clown ducked down by his side.

"You okay, kid?"

Kyle didn't answer. Bren's heart raced so fast words sounded like they came from a distance. "Kyle?" he called gently, touching the boy's shoulder.

"We need a medic," the clown shouted, waving.

"No."

They both heard the word. Trent had rushed over and knelt next to Kyle, too. So did another rodeo official.

Kyle's eyes opened. "No medic."

"Did you hit your head?" the bullfighter asked.

"My leg," Kyle moaned.

"Can you get up?" Trent asked because he could see nothing beneath the boy's chaps.

Kyle nodded, but when he went to move, he gasped in pain. Bren knew it had to hurt. Kyle was a tough kid.

"Take it easy," the rodeo official said, tipping his straw hat back. "You don't need to move."

"Wanna get up."

Kyle's eyes were wide with something close to fear. His gaze snagged on Bren's, and the way he looked at him, as if he sought comfort or reassurance, it made Bren's throat close up.

"We should get a medic in here."

"No," Kyle said, thrusting himself up.

"Whoa, whoa, whoa," he warned, trying to keep the boy down, but the kid wouldn't have it. Beneath the cage of his steer-riding helmet, Kyle's face went pale, but by gum, if he didn't manage to climb to his feet. Trent helped him. So did the bullfighter. Bren stood up, too, feeling such a sense of helplessness as Kyle hobbled out of the arena it nearly made him sick.

Lauren.

He turned toward the grandstands. He knew Lauren was up there. No doubt she was already on her way to the chutes.

"Ladies and gentlemen," said the announcer, "give Kyle Danners a round of applause, would you? And wait, check out his score. Man, this is going to be tough to beat—eighty-eight for his ride on Exterminator."

Kyle should have been jumping up and down for joy, but when they got behind the chutes, he could see tears in the kid's eyes. "It hurts," he said to him, not to Trent—his hero—but to him.

"Let's take a look at it, then," he said, kneeling down in front of him and unzipping his chaps.

Kyle propped himself up against the back of the steer pen. Trent helped to lift his jeans above his boots.

"Stepped on," Trent pronounced.

Sure enough, they could see the double lines of a hoof mark on Kyle's shin. "Gonna need to get that x-rayed."

"Will I be okay?" Kyle asked Bren.

"Of course you will be." He forced a smile on his face. "Been stepped on more times than I can count."

"Congratulations," said one of the boy's competitors. "That was a great ride."

"Thanks," Kyle said.

"I'll go get my rental car," Trent said. "Be easier to get in and out of than a truck."

Bren nodded, helping the boy to remove his helmet. Kyle's hair was sticking up with sweat and he had a scared-little-boy look on face. Bren wanted to hug him. He wanted to wrap him in his arms and hold him tight. He wanted to tell him to never ride steers again. The emotions coursing through him were feelings he'd never felt before and it baffled the hell out of him.

"Kyle!" Lauren cried. "Are you okay?"

She must have run all the way down from the stands. She pressed herself up against the boards of the chutes.

"Got stepped on, Mom."

He saw Lauren's eyes close for a moment and he knew she tried to gather her emotions. "You shouldn't move. We need to immobilize it immediately. Somebody get a stretcher."

"Mom. Relax. I'm okay."

"You don't know that. You came off hard."

For the first time Bren realized her stress about Kyle riding came from a whole other direction than most moms'. She'd spent years in college studying all the horrible things that could go wrong. No wonder she was a stress mess.

"You should probably have it x-rayed," Bren said. "Just in case."

Alana had come up next to her and placed a comforting hand on Lauren's shoulder. "He'll be okay. He's tough."

He was. Bren had to admit, the kid held himself together, more stoic now that he was in front of his mother. He didn't cry. Didn't moan. Didn't whine about the pain. He just gave his mom a nod and in as grown-up a voice as Bren had ever heard said, "Let's go get it x-rayed, if you want, but I'm sure it's okay."

Attaboy, he silently told him when their eyes connected. Kyle tried to smile, but Bren could tell it was false, and in that moment he realized the truth.

He loved the kid.

He didn't know how it'd happened in such a short amount of time, but the surge of emotion he felt as he stared down into the brave boy's eyes must be what fathers felt for their own children.

It nearly brought him to tears.

"Ms. Danners."

Lauren shot up from the seat where she'd been sitting next to Kyle as he lay on a paper-coated gurney in one of six partitioned "rooms" in the Norco emergency ward. "Looks like we're in the clear. There's no break."

Lauren wanted to fall back into her chair. Or pass out. She didn't know which.

"You mean I'm okay?" Kyle asked.

"Yup." The doctor took in the rest of their entourage: Bren, Jax, Trent and Alana. "And good job with the brace, Ms. Danners. If Kyle's leg had been broken, it could have really saved him from damaging it further. So often I see these cowboy types come in all full of bluster and 'I'm all rights' and they just mess themselves up more. Good to see someone can be a voice of reason."

She glanced around the room to see how the comment was taken because she had a feeling Jax and Trent and Bren had just been insulted. "Thank you."

"One of the PAs said you're studying to be a nurse?"

The doctor stared at her so intently she felt herself blush. If she didn't know better, she'd swear he was flirting. "I'm actually graduating this fall."

"Oh, yeah? What college?"

"Can I go home now?"

They all froze, Kyle clearly at the end of his patience, her son looking tiny in the big bed, his body covered by a thin blue blanket, eyes wide with...was it disgruntlement?

"Of course."

She released Kyle's hand and held it out to the doctor. "Thank you."

"You're welcome." He smiled at Kyle, barely glancing in everyone else's direction. "Maybe we'll see you again one day."

He *was* flirting with her. "Maybe."

They all watched the doctor leave and there was no mistaking the way he looked back at her, his mouth tipped up on one side. Lauren didn't know whether to feel flattered or amused.

"Wow," Jax said once the doctor was out of earshot. "I think you have a new friend."

"Oh, please."

"I'm surprised he didn't ask for your number," Alana said with a grin.

"You guys, stop."

"He was flirting with you, Mom," Kyle said, swinging his leg over the side of the bed with a wince. "We all saw it."

"I'm sure he was just being kind because I'm your mom."

"Hah," Kyle said, and then he looked around. "What am I going to wear?"

They'd left his chaps in the rental car, had cut his pants off his leg earlier. Thankfully, his boots hadn't been sacrificed, but that still left them in a dilemma.

"Relax," Alana said. "Fortunately, or maybe it should be sadly, I have a lot of experience with this. They'll bring you hospital pants if you ask."

"Hospital pants?" Kyle said, wrinkling his nose.

"It doesn't matter what you wear on your way out," Trent said. "You'll be in a wheelchair anyway. They always insist."

"Oh, yeah?"

Lauren could tell Kyle had let go of his fear and had moved on to enjoying the moment. She glanced at Bren and knew he felt the same way as she did. His relief that Kyle would be all right was evident in the way the brackets around his mouth had loosened. In the way he slowly stood, a small smile tipping the edges of his lips as he stared down at her son, and in that gaze she saw something that made her breath catch and made her realize that before her stood a man who cared—truly cared—about her and her son.

She had to look away.

"I'll go tell them we need pants," Alana said.

"And I'll go with her," Trent said.

"Guess I'll tag along," Bren said, heading out. She watched him go, torn, but in the end, she shot Kyle and Jax a reassuring smile before saying, "Be right back."

He was right behind Alana and Trent, but she stopped him with a "Bren, wait."

He swung back toward her. She caught Alana's gaze, asking without words for a private moment. The woman smiled. Not that it would be very private. They were in the main emergency area. Beyond the curtain sat a long counter with printers and computers and laptops manned by half a dozen staff members. Everyone ignored them, busy with whatever crises they were trying to solve. That would be her next year, except she'd be at the bottom rung of the ladder. Night shifts. Weekend shifts. Crazy schedule. Crazy life. No time for a man.

"Thank you," she said when he came back to stand in front of her.

"Don't thank me," he said. "Trent and Alana were just as helpful."

"I know, but it's not just today—it's…everything."

He nodded and she could tell he was truly touched by her gratitude.

"I'm sorry we ruined your plans for a barbecue."

He grimaced. "I forgot about that."

"Me, too, but I don't think it's a good idea. I should probably get Kyle home and his leg on ice."

He nodded. "I'm just glad he's okay."

"And I've been thinking about your question."

His gaze sharpened like the tip of a pencil. He focused all that passion, all that interest, all that dedication on her and it made her want to wiggle.

"If the offer's still open, I'll go out with you next week." It was the least she could do, she told herself. She owed him dinner. "But it'll be my treat."

"You don't have to pay."

"I want to. Please?"

She could tell he didn't want to agree, but she could also tell he would take what he could get. "Great." And then he turned away and she felt strangely deflated.

"About time."

She turned to find her brother peering through the curtain, his brown eyes full of amusement. "You took longer to decide on that than Congress did to ratify the Constitution."

"Hah-hah-hah." She made a face at him. "Very funny."

It was a charity dinner. That was all. Nothing more to it.

At least, that's what she told herself.

Chapter Twelve

"Where are my shoes?" Lauren tossed one pair of shoes after another—mostly different types of tennis shoes—toward the base of her bed. "I swear this closet is too big."

"Mom," Kyle said from behind her. "Relax. It's just a date."

So speaketh the child. As if he knew what it was like to go out on a date with someone.

"It's not a date," she quickly corrected. "It's just dinner."

Her son snorted. She shot him a glare, but who was she trying to kid? She'd been telling herself all week it was no big deal. That it was a purely platonic dinner, but she'd realized about Thursday she was being an idiot. It didn't help that it was Valentine's Day. For some reason that had changed things. Now she was a complete mess, a part of wondering if she should cancel, another part of her, the feminine side that wanted to feel special and like a woman again, wanted to look her best. And thus her frantic search for the perfect dress and now the shoes she knew she had somewhere. It was Valentine's Day weekend, and by gum, she was going out on a date.

"I know they're in here, darn it."

She was in search of a single pair of high-heel shoes that she'd almost thrown out when she'd unpacked a few weeks ago. Something had made her stop, some forlorn hope that maybe she wasn't a complete emotional mess and she'd be brave enough to go out on a date at some point in her life. And now look. Only she couldn't find the darn shoes.

"Did you look up on the shelf?"

She straightened suddenly. "That's right."

She had to drag a chair to reach all way to the back, and sure enough, there they were.

"Eureka." She did a little happy dance with the shoes in her hands.

Kyle stared at her as if she'd lost her mind. "Calm down."

She glanced at the clock. She'd spent fifteen minutes finding the shoes. Bren would be here any moment now.

Her stomach rolled like it was a wave crashing onto shore.

It's not a date, she told herself.

It's a date, she admitted. She'd better just dive in and go whole hog.

"You're going to look pretty, Mom."

She glanced at the red dress she'd yet to don and wondered if he was right. It'd been so long since she'd worn something nice for a man. She wasn't sure she remembered how. Bren had told her to dress up. That he was taking her someplace nice. She'd done her best, but she'd given up on styling her hair earlier, leaving it hanging down her back. She might have gone overboard on her makeup, though. She wasn't sure how much to put on and her bathroom light was so bright...

"Mom!"

She straightened suddenly, turning toward her son. "What?"

"He's here."

"What?"

She raced to the front of the house. She peeked out the front window, and sure enough, she could see the dark outline of his truck.

"Damn." She ran back to her room. "Stall him."

"Mom. You're starting to freak me out."

"Just do it."

Someone knocked. Kyle lifted a brow.

"Now," she whispered.

Off he went with a long, drawn-out sigh. She closed the door, leaned up against it and breathed deeply. Heavens to Betsy, this was harder than it looked. What had it been? Eleven? Twelve years? She tried to remember how long she and Paul had dated before they'd been married. Whatever it was, it'd been a long, long time ago, and thoughts of Paul really didn't help matters.

She pushed away from the door, determined to look her best, but a few minutes later, as she studied herself in the mirror, her courage failed.

You can do this. It's just one date. On Valentine's Day. Millions of women are doing the same thing right now. Go on. Have fun.

For once she decided to listen to the little voice, because when it came right down to it, she was tired of being tired, of feeling like an overworked mom. Tonight she wanted to feel like a woman.

The look on Bren's face when she finally emerged from her room told her she just might have succeeded.

"Wow," Kyle said. "Mom. You look...*awesome*!"

She flicked the short skirt back and forth. "Thanks."

Bren looked pretty good, too, in his black button-down and solid dark blue tie. His black slacks matched his shirt and she wondered if he had a jacket out in his truck. But then she noticed the look in his eyes and it made her freeze for a moment, her thoughts spinning furiously away. That look...that's what she'd wanted to see, she suddenly realized. She'd wanted to light a fire. To make him look at her like she was the most beautiful thing he'd ever seen. It didn't matter if she was actually pretty. She just wanted *him* to see her that way.

And he did.

"I should have worn my badge," she heard him say. "I'm going to need my gun to keep the men away."

She turned the same color as her dress, but that was okay. She ran her hands down the front of the silk fabric. It was tight through the hips but then flared to just above the knees. She'd been concerned it might be a little too sexy, but what the heck. It made her feel good.

"You ready to go?"

He nodded, stepped back to the door, seeming to be bemused for a moment, but then he recovered himself and she thought she spotted something like concern in his eyes. Only it faded quickly and she wondered if she'd imagined it.

"You're heading straight over to Uncle Jax's, right?"

"Yes, Mom."

"Okay, well, I'm not sure how long we'll be out, but you have my cell phone number, in case you need me."

"Mo-om," Kyle said. "Stop talking. Go on. Leave."

He stared up at her with such endearing impatience that she wanted to bend down and kiss him, but she knew that would only embarrass him in front of Bren.

So she grabbed her purse, gave him a smile and headed out to Bren's truck.

In for a penny, in for a pound.

HE COULDN'T KEEP his eyes off her. If he'd thought she looked cute in pigtails, that was nothing compared to the way she looked with her hair down around her shoulders and in that sexy red dress.

Ai-yai-yai.

She was still too young for him, but he was having trouble remembering that. If his campaign consultant, Jerry Blaylock, saw his date, he'd probably throw a fit. To hell with it. Nobody would see them in an elite coastal restaurant. Nobody would care that a man with a bit of gray in his hair escorted a brown-haired beauty. Hell, even if people did, he didn't care what they thought at the moment.

He glanced at her legs as he started his truck.

To hell with Jerry.

"Where are we going?" she asked.

"I'm taking you to a restaurant on the coast. Friend of mine owns it—otherwise we'd have never gotten a table on such short notice—and you're not paying for it."

She shot him a look. "But this is my thank-you dinner."

"This is not a thank-you dinner." She wanted to argue, but he cut her off with "You do not wear a dress like that for a thank-you dinner."

She blushed. He could tell. "My treat, and, by the way—" he reached into the backseat of his truck "—these are for you." He handed her the dozen roses he'd picked up.

"They're beautiful." He could see the pleased surprise in her eyes. The late-afternoon sun perfectly caught the expression on her face. She dipped her nose in them, inhaling the rose fragrance. "Thank you."

Her reaction made his hurried stop at the florist worth it. He'd been worried it might make him late, but he'd ended up cooling his heels anyway, though she was worth the wait.

"I probably should have given them to you at the house." He'd been nervous. Like a kid about to ride his first bull. He'd sat out front for what felt like an hour but was probably more like seconds, all so he could collect himself.

"No. Now is great. Honestly. It's been so long since anyone's gotten me flowers…"

She let her words trail off and he knew she felt the same way he did. Out of his depth. Anxious. Maybe even a little afraid.

Of what?

He'd kept asking himself that question the whole time he'd gotten dressed. What was it about her that made him so fearful? He'd been a bachelor for his whole life. Just because he was going out with her didn't mean that would change. And what a strange thought to have, anyway.

"Is Kyle feeling better?"

He'd been restricted from riding anything with four legs, at least until his bruises healed. He hadn't taken the news well, but they'd be back at it next week.

"He's feeling well enough to complain every five minutes."

"Never met a kid who loved riding steers as much as him, except maybe me."

She nodded as she looked out the window, and Bren tried not to keep peeking glances at her long legs. It made him feel even more like a lecherous old man. But she wasn't that much younger than him. Heck, in another twenty years the age gap would hardly make a difference.

Twenty years?

What was he doing thinking that far ahead?

"Alana told me you were good." Their gazes connected as he waited for the ranch gate to swing open, the angle of the sun causing a shadow to drag beneath it. "*Really* good, but that you quit."

He felt his heart do something strange when he admitted that, yeah, he was kind of thinking ahead. "Did she tell you why?"

"Something about horses and Las Vegas and a midnight ride."

He thought back to that night, and just like it always did, it made him a little sick. "I could have killed someone."

"You and the other guys."

His grip tightened on the wheel, but then he forced himself to loosen it. "Still, it was a wake-up call."

Her hazel eyes took on the shine of a golden ring. "A lot of guys would have ignored that call."

"Some of them did."

"Why not you?"

He'd never been asked that question before, and for a moment he thought about sidestepping it, but something about the warmth in her eyes, about the way she stared at him so boldly—as if daring him to look deep inside—it made him want to answer with the cold, hard truth.

"My dad was a drunk."

She didn't seem surprised. All she did was nod.

"And his dad before him." The gate had finished opening, and so he pulled forward, driving without really thinking about it. "I thought I could control it. My dad drank because he hated his life. He worked for an asphalt company. Big-equipment operator. Good money. Crap job. He'd come home from work tired, hot, sweaty, in a bad mood. And so he drank. A lot. And I hated him for it. I couldn't wait to get out of the house. I found bull riding and that was my ticket out. But I would be different, I told myself. I wouldn't drink. Ever."

"If only it were that easy."

"No kidding, right?"

He shook his head in disgust. "At first I beat it. All through high school rodeo I never touched a drink. Then I started bull riding and we'd go out on the weekends and I'd have a drink here and there. Everyone called me a prude. One drink a weekend turned into two. I told myself it was no big deal. I had it under control."

"But you didn't."

He nodded as he turned onto the main road. "That night, when we took those horses out, I can't honestly say how many drinks I had. When I sobered up, it made me think about what I was doing with my life. And how, in the end, my life didn't mean squat. I wasn't curing cancer. I wasn't making the world a better place. I was just riding bulls. We could have killed someone that night. *I* could have killed someone. For what? A good time and some fame and glory? What a crock. So I quit."

He could feel her stare, glanced over at her.

"You chose sobriety over notoriety."

He'd never really thought about it that way. "I guess so."

Her hand reached out for his, covering it. "That's an amazing thing to do."

"Not really. Not when you consider what I'd grown up with."

"Was it bad?"

"Bad enough."

He didn't want to think about the fights his parents had when he was growing up. The yelling. His mom begging his father to stop. The dozens of times she'd left him, always dragging him along, only to go back. That wasn't a life he'd wanted.

"I enlisted in the army the next day. Went into law enforcement and then became town sheriff. I've dedicated my life to helping others and it's a much better use of my time."

Her hand squeezed his own. "Do you miss it?" She smiled softly. "The bull riding?"

He swallowed. It felt like a ton of bricks landed on his belly.

"Every day of my life." Her hazel eyes looked into his own and there was so much admiration in them that he lost the ability to speak for a moment.

"It was a good decision."

Her hand squeezed his again, and he knew that if he squeezed back, he was committing to something bigger than himself. Tonight. This date. Wherever it was going, it was bigger than anything he'd ever done before. Bigger than bull riding. Bigger than the army. Bigger than being the town sheriff. That should scare the hell out of him.

It didn't.

Chapter Thirteen

He took her to the most beautiful place on earth. An old farmhouse nestled atop a grass-covered bluff, the whitewashed home having been converted into a five-star restaurant. She knew the instant she sat down it would be good.

"Bren," said a man wearing a white smock and one of those puffy chef's hats that always looked slightly ridiculous. "You made it."

"We did." He turned to her. "Lauren, this is Leland."

He couldn't be much older than Bren, she thought, smiling at the dark-haired man with the light blue eyes. He took her hand and, in the most gallant of manners, bent down to kiss it, his hat nearly poking her in the face.

"Charmed," he said in a French accent.

"Oh, please," Bren said, shaking his head at his friend. "It's all an act. Leland worked in the mess hall back when we were in the Army."

The twinkle turned on Bren. "Shh," he said, glancing around the crowded restaurant. "Don't give me away."

He seemed nice and she was happy to meet one of Bren's friends. The man turned his attention back to her. "I am pleased to have such beauty sampling my food," he said in his fake accent.

She snorted.

Leland leaned in toward Bren. "Where'd you find her? She's a bit young for you, isn't she?"

She happened to be staring right at Bren when the words were said, and so she saw him freeze, but for only a moment, and for the first time she wondered if he was sensitive to their age difference. She'd never given it much thought.

Bren had obviously prickled. "She's a fourth-year nursing student about to graduate with her RN."

She loved him in that instant. He said the words with such pride that she felt a lump form in her throat.

"Beauty *and* brains." Leland smiled at her again. "Lucky you." He patted Bren on the back. "Enjoy your meal."

And he was off, leaving them sitting at their little table up against a glass window that overlooked the ocean and a low-hanging sun.

"He's a character," she said, admiring the single red rose that sat in a small crystal vase, the only sign that it was Valentine's Day. Its fragrance filled the air.

"He's one of the best chefs in the nation."

"Really?"

A woman wearing a black apron came over, a wide smile on her face as she poured her some wine, but not for Bren, she noticed. Clearly Leland knew Bren well.

"Compliments of the chef," she said, disappearing as silently as she'd come.

"Do you mind?" she asked.

"Not at all. Leland might be offended if you don't drink, actually. He's a nut about matching wine with a meal. We won't be allowed to order, either. He'll choose for us."

"Amazing," she said, but she was talking about the wine. It was delicious. "How did he go from the army to this?" She motioned with her hands to the white linen and crystal glasses.

"He won a cooking show."

She couldn't stop the huff of laughter. "What?"

Bren smiled, too. "He was a cook the whole time he was in the army. When he hung up his camo, he tried out for one of those cooking shows and he got on. The rest, as they say, is history."

"From mess hall to master chef."

"Something like that."

They chatted about his eight years in the military. He'd been a member of the Army Special Forces, she learned, the Green Berets. He'd been highly decorated, too, although she'd had to pry that bit of information out of him. Their food arrived later, although how much later she had no idea, and the beef Wellington was so good she could have died right then and been happy.

"You look like you're in heaven."

She nodded. "I was just thinking that." She pointed with her fork. "Your friend's talents were wasted in the army."

"Not anymore."

She stared at the sun, admiring the way it turned the ocean the same color as the sky—fiery red—and how the waves seemed to twinkle beneath it.

"You couldn't have timed this more perfectly."

"You can thank Leland for the dinner reservation."

She nodded. "I will."

He held her gaze. "Happy Valentine's Day."

Lauren felt the hairs on her neck begin to tingle. Suddenly she didn't feel like eating. It didn't matter how good the food was. The look in his eyes was ravenous and it made her ravenous, too.

"How is it?"

They both jumped. Leland stared down at them in amusement.

"Fantastic," she said.

"Good." He turned toward Bren while their waitress poured Bren some coffee. "You still doing that thing for dessert?"

Bren touched his napkin to his chin. "I am."

"I'll have Glenda package it up, then."

"Package what up?" she asked as Leland walked away.

"We're doing dessert down on the beach."

Her toes curled into her high-heeled shoes.

"I have blankets and pillows in the truck."

She knew what he planned then, and it had nothing to do with eating dessert. She could say no, she told herself. He would understand if she asked to go home instead. She knew that. Bren was an honorable man. But she didn't want to say no. Maybe it was the wine and the amazing dinner or the sunset and his soft smile as he relayed funny rodeo stories from his past, but she didn't want the evening to end.

"Sounds like fun."

His eyes heated up, and she knew she hadn't mistaken the intention in his gaze. Glenda came up with a white bag. He never looked up.

"Check," was all he said.

HE COULDN'T GET her out of there fast enough. All through dinner he'd been fantasizing about peeling the straps of her dress off her shoulders and wondering what she'd taste like.

"Bren!"

He froze.

"Our illustrious sheriff and…"

Bren turned and faced city council member Frank Farrell, a man who'd never been friendly in all the years he'd been sheriff of Via Del Caballo. He clearly tried to place Lauren, but his thoughts were just as clearly consumed by her cleavage based on the way his gaze shifted downward and stayed there.

"Lauren," she said. "Lauren Danners."

And all the romance went out of the evening because Frank's wife stared at Lauren as if she were a stripper at a preschool. Her gaze swept her up and down, her lips, already too thin, pinching together. The coldness in her gaze matched the ice of her blue eyes.

"Well, now," Frank said with his best Southern accent, an affectation that drove Bren nuts. The man was a native Californian, but he loved to wear cowboy hats and boots and act like a bona fide rancher when he was anything but. "I don't believe we've ever met."

"I don't believe we have, either." Lauren's smile was kind and friendly and he admired that about her. Surely she noticed the lasciviousness in Frank's gaze. The man's wife sure did. But she held her chin high.

"And you must be Bren's younger sister."

Okay, now, look, he wanted to say. There was no way in hell Lauren was his sister. Not when she was on his arm and coming out of a restaurant on Valentine's Day. The man knew it, too. He was just making a veiled reference to the age gap.

"*Way* younger sister," he thought he heard Frank's wife mutter.

Lauren's eyes zeroed in on the woman.

"No, I'm not," she said before he could shut them both up with a rude comment. She turned back toward him, long dark hair flipping over one shoulder. "Are these your grandparents, Bren? The ones you were telling me about earlier?"

He about choked on the words he was about to unleash on Frank's wife. It took him a second to gather his thoughts, but then he said, "No, no," playing along. "These aren't them."

"Too bad." She smiled at the couple, even though there was no way on earth either one of them could be considered old enough to have grandchildren Bren's age. Frank's wife glared daggers because she understood all too well that things had been turned around on them. Bren didn't care. He just wanted out of there.

"Nice to see you," he told them both, tipping his head and wishing he had on his cowboy hat. "Enjoy your dinner."

He waited until they were out of earshot before whispering, "Sorry about that."

"What jerks," Lauren said as they walked toward his truck. "Why were they looking at me like you're a choirboy and I'm trying to corrupt you or something? Is this dress really that bad?"

He didn't trust himself to speak for a moment because it upset him that those two losers had her doubting her own looks. "Your dress is perfect. That was all aimed at me."

And their age gap.

"Who is he?"

He didn't want to think about that. Not now. "He's on the city council." They'd reached his truck and he swiped a hand through his hair. Talk about a good evening gone bad. He hated that A-hole for dragging Lauren into his political agenda. "He thinks I don't do enough as sheriff. That I'm a figurehead, not a leader. He's been my biggest opponent when it comes to staying sheriff. It's because of Frank Farrell that I'm always having to watch my back. He's never liked me since the moment I won my first election and he'll never like me so long as I keep being sheriff."

She looked just as perturbed as he felt and the fight drained out of him. What a remarkable woman she was. It'd taken her 2.9 seconds to reason out that she'd been insulted and 1.9 seconds to dish it back.

He cupped her face with his hands. He saw her eyes widen, saw her mouth press together for an instant before her lips relaxed and he felt a nearly irresistible urge to kiss her. In front of God and everybody.

But he didn't kiss her.

"He's a jerk and I'm not going to let him ruin our night."

Those soft lips smiled. "Neither am I."

He didn't have time to analyze why he held back, because the sun was about to go down and he wanted to be on the beach before that happened.

"Come on." He turned to his truck. Inside, he'd stashed a blanket, which he grabbed after he handed their special dessert to Lauren. "There's a path to the right of the restaurant."

"As long as we don't have to bump into those people again."

"We won't."

Don't let it ruin your night. But it was impossible not to think about. Lauren hadn't been exposed to his political life. She'd never had to watch him run for office. It could get nasty, and Frank Farrell had just played into his worst fear. The man wouldn't hesitate to use Lauren's age against him somehow.

What did it matter?

He'd just had an amazing dinner with an amazing woman who was twice the person of Frank or Victoria Farrell. A single mom who'd lost her husband. Who'd put herself through college and raised a fine young man. To hell with them. But he knew, he just knew, they were probably watching them as they walked toward the beach.

"You're going to get sand in your boots."

He turned back to her. They'd just crossed over a big dune and he realized they couldn't be seen through the glass of the restaurant. She stood there, framed by the sky behind, a breeze blowing her hair back, the sound of the ocean booming in the distance, and he knew he would never forget the moment.

She was, in a word, beautiful.

"I was just thinking I should take them off."

"You should." She held up her own shoes, smiling. Lord. Could she look any more young? Such a girlish grin and such a pretty smile. The sun had gone down to the point that the earth chipped away at its roundness, tingeing everything around them red. In her dress and with her dark hair streaked by golden light, she looked like a Greek goddess come down from above.

"Man, you're beautiful."

Her mouth dropped open a bit and he could tell it'd been a long time since a man had told her that.

"Thank you."

He walked toward her and he knew he was going to kiss her and that the kiss might change everything, but he didn't care. He had to taste her right then, maybe as a way to convince himself she was real.

Her eyes grew wide. He set the blanket down. She stared up at him. He cupped her chin. She still held the bag with the dessert, but he heard it drop just before his lips connected with hers.

God help him.

He'd known how she would taste. He remembered the feel of her lips. Nothing could have prepared him for the jolt to his soul when she yielded to his mouth, her lips nuzzling, then opening a bit, then nuzzling him again, and he knew if she opened her mouth, if she let him taste her like he'd wanted to taste her for weeks now, he'd really lose it.

He pulled back.

She followed him forward a bit, her eyes snapping open.

"I didn't buy a dessert to let it go to waste."

"We don't have to eat it here."

He froze. "What do you mean?"

He watched as her lips tried out words, discarded them, then tried them again until she finally said, "We could go back to your place."

Her words were like the jab of a hot wire. They electrified every nerve ending in his body, charging his blood and making him want to do things he hadn't done in, well, a long while.

"Are you sure?"

She lifted her chin, swallowed and—ah, hell—looked even more young.

"Yes."

Don't do it. Don't say yes. Wait until after election, when men like Frank Farrell can say whatever they want instead of trying to make this thing with Lauren work against him.

But he knew he was a lost cause. He'd been lost ever since he'd seen her walk out in the red dress. And then later, when he'd watched her eat, loving the way her eyes lit up and her body gave a little wiggle when she tasted something she really liked.

"Bren?"

She'd lost her self-confidence while he'd stood there waffling. He could see in the way her shoulders sagged and the sparkle began to fade from her eyes. She had the wrong idea about his hesitation.

"Let's go."

She smiled softly. "Okay."

Chapter Fourteen

What are you doing? What are you doing? What are you doing?

The words were a litany in her head. She hadn't been with a man in years. Heck, she hadn't been with anyone other than her husband in well over a decade. What if she'd forgotten to shave? Had she shaved? Darn it, she couldn't remember.

I've changed my mind.

The words hovered on her lips. Two things stopped her. One, she'd wanted him to kiss her since the moment she'd spotted him standing near her front door, eyes sparking to life when he'd seen her in the red dress. Two, the look on Frank Farrell's face. It was as if he didn't approve of her, which was ridiculous. What wasn't there to approve of? Was it the red dress? Or was it the age difference? If so, that was ridiculous. She wasn't that much younger than Bren. Okay, maybe he was a little older, but only a little. Bren was sensitive about it, though, so she would just prove to him there was no reason to be. She wouldn't let Frank Farrell ruin their night.

"I can't say what it's going to look like inside," he

told her as they pulled into his drive. "I mean, it could be a complete mess."

She glanced over at him. It was dark, the lights of the dash illuminating his face. "I don't care."

And that was the other reason why she stuck to her guns. She didn't care. She was tired of worrying about what other people thought. Tired of watching all the other women at school go out on dates and have fun and actually *enjoy* life. She wanted that, too.

At least for a night.

"I'm sure it'll be fine."

But was she talking about his house being clean? Or herself being fine? She didn't know and frankly didn't care. Even by the light of his dash she could see the heat in his gaze. It hadn't waned since they left the beach, the tension in his truck bubbling closer to the surface the nearer they were to his house until, like a vat of liquid desire, it spilled over.

He opened his door. She watched for a moment because even though she'd made her decision, it didn't mean her heart didn't pound and that she had the courage to follow through, because, darn it all, it'd been so long. What if he was disappointed? What if he took one look at her baby belly and changed his mind? What if...

Honey, this is a man we're talking about, said the little voice.

True, but...

He was coming around to her side of the truck. He'd done that earlier, too. He'd let her out at the restaurant. A courtly gentleman with the softest of lips and the sweetest of eyes, and with every step her heart began to beat even harder.

This is it. This is it. This is it.

He opened the door. Courage deserted her. He held out a hand. She took a deep breath.

"It's okay."

It would be, she reassured herself. She needed to have faith. He would never treat her as Paul had treated her. She knew that with the same certainty that she knew the sun would rise.

She slipped from the truck.

He caught her. She used his forearms to steady her. He scooped her up into his arms.

"Bren," she murmured.

He nuzzled her neck for a split second and her whole body quaked in response.

She didn't know when he started walking or even how he kept nuzzling her hair and her ear while managing to hold her close. All she knew was one minute she was at the truck and the next she was slowly sliding down the length of his body while he flicked on a light.

He had a nice house.

That, too, registered on some level. As did the wide-open space and the high ceilings and thick wooden beams above. She used a hand against his chest to steady herself and beneath it she could feel the pounding of his heart and it surprised her. Their gazes connected.

"Are you nervous, too?" she heard herself ask.

"You have no idea."

Yes, she did, she was about to say, but then he kissed her. It wasn't the tentative kiss at the arena, nor the soft kiss at the beach. This was a carnal "I want you and you want me" no-holds-barred kiss and that made her soul sing, *Yes!* Her hands drifted upward as his mouth teased her lips until at last she opened herself to him fully, tasting him for the first time.

And she knew.

They were perfect for each other. He had a taste to him, a tangy essence that made her toes curl and her nerve endings fire and her fingers grasp behind his neck, and it was like nothing she'd ever experienced before. He changed the angle of his head. She opened even farther and tasted the coffee he'd had with his dinner and a hint of the raspberries in the glaze that'd been drizzled on his duck. Beneath it all she tasted something else, too. Something that was uniquely him—a sweetness that made her want to kiss him all night.

His fingers found the straps of her dress. She shivered as he tugged them down and then moaned because he pulled his lips away and then groaned when his mouth lightly nipped the spot where the fabric had been. His other hand slid up her side, his thumb finding the curve of her breast, and she went weak when he touched her there, her head lolling back. That seemed to be an invitation for his mouth to move upward, his lips nibbling her as he followed the line of her neck. He suckled her. His hands squeezed her. She about died right there and then.

"Can I take you to bed?"

She heard the words from a distance, opened her eyes. He had pulled back enough so that she could see into his eyes.

"We can stop right here if you want."

How different he was from Paul, who would take whatever he wanted. That was why she hadn't been with a man in years. She'd been scared.

She wasn't afraid of Bren. Far from it.

So she smiled softly and answered from the heart. "Yes."

His hands shook so bad he didn't know if he'd be able to do much more than kiss her.

"I apologize if there are clothes strewn everywhere."

There would be more clothes, soon. He almost stumbled; instead he led her down the long hall that ran parallel to the front of the house, the tall, narrow windows giving him a glimpse of the outside. His room was at the end and when he flicked the light switch on, he breathed a sigh of relief. Not as bad as he'd thought.

"Your house is beautiful."

He pulled her through the door, back into his arms, staring deep into her eyes as he said, "Not as beautiful as you," and meaning every word.

He saw it again then, the uncertainty that'd been plaguing her gaze all night. What was it that concerned her? He'd tried to take it slow. Lord, out by his front door, it'd been all he could do not to push her up against it and take her then and there. Instead something told him to hold back. To let her set the pace, but damn it, the look in her eyes nearly killed him.

"What?" he heard himself ask. "What is it that has you looking so worried? Is it me?"

Her eyes widened. He nearly groaned when her tongue slipped out when she licked her lips. "No." And he could tell by the directness of her gaze that she meant every word. "It's not you at all." She took a deep breath. "It's me."

"You?"

"Bren. It's been forever. As in years and years. And I'm not young anymore. I've gained weight. Had a kid—"

"Are you kidding?" He closed the distance between them. "You're perfect."

"No, I'm not." She shook her head. "See this?" She motioned toward her waist. "Spandex. And my breasts? Push-up bra. My legs look smooth because of panty hose and my belly hasn't been flat since I had Kyle."

Insecurity. That's what he'd been seeing in her eyes and it made his insides do something funny. He almost smiled. Almost. Instead he touched her shoulders, one hand moving upward so he could tip her chin.

"When you were standing atop the dune at the beach, I thought to myself you were the most beautiful woman I've ever seen."

He saw her eyes fill with tears. For some strange reason it set his own eyes to burning. How could such a beautiful woman lack confidence?

Paul.

He knew it in that instant. Knew that her brother had been right. She'd been in a miserable marriage. But she stuck it out, and it'd left scars. Deep ones.

"You're perfect." He gently pulled her against him. "Do you feel what you do to me?"

Her eyes had flared, but then just as quickly the fire faded. "I do, but I'm telling you, without my clothes…"

"Shhh." He used a thumb to silence her. "Just shhhh."

And then he kissed her again. He would show her without words how beautiful she was to him, how exquisitely perfect and desirable and just plain sexy. She still felt stiff in his arms, but he was patient, increasing the pressure of his lips until she opened for him and the sweet taste of her made him groan. She was honeysuckle wine. The caramel in the center of chocolate. The whipped cream atop a cherry pie.

He didn't remember doing it, but somehow he ended up pressing her against his bedroom door. He placed a palm against it, holding himself up, because kissing her was like riding down rapids on a hot summer day. Exhilarating and wild and just a little bit crazy.

She suckled his tongue.

Their tongues twined and twisted and he was in a frenzy of desire, lifting his hips and then sliding down again, recreating the same movement in her mouth, his whole body tightening and hardening until...

"Damn." He all but gasped the word. He tossed his head back, gulped in air. "You're killing me."

He tipped her chin up, a gesture that had become near and dear to him in recent weeks. Her eyes were huge and nearly black.

"Do you?"

She said, "I think so."

He still breathed raggedly. Still felt rock hard and on the verge of something that was bigger than him and that should scare him but strangely didn't.

"I want to make love to you," he said with brutal honesty. "But we can end this night right here and right now if that's what you want." His thumb stroked the side of her jaw. "I would understand."

He saw the indecision in her expression, but he also saw the sizzle deep in her hazel eyes, the same electrical dance of fire that played havoc with his skin, leaving the hair standing on end.

"I don't want to leave."

"Then stay."

"Okay."

Chapter Fifteen

He's going to see you naked.

So? He obviously doesn't care.

But he's never seen you naked before.

He was about to, she thought, standing in his arms, her heart beating so hard she was sure he could feel it. The realization made her feel as if she were about to jump off the edge of a building, one fifty stories high. She would get to see him naked, too. And he would do things to her. Naughty things. That she could imagine, as well, because if she were honest with herself, she'd already imagined it on more than one sleepless night. She might have fought the attraction between them, but her subconscious didn't. Oh, no. It indulged in the sexiest of fantasies and at least one of them, she knew, was about to come true.

"Look," he whispered, his breath brushing the shell of her ear. He pointed and she realized that from where she stood, she could see herself in the bathroom mirror. See the both of them. The room was spacious but not dark. The wood floors reflected a golden light that seemed to come from above the vanity, but she couldn't be sure. All she knew was that she could see him there.

And her. And that it was both strange and exhilarating to be with someone other than Paul.

"Watch," he whispered next.

She tensed when she felt his hands at the back of her dress, where the zipper was. The pads of his fingers brushed her skin. She froze as he slowly, oh so inexorably, separated the metal teeth.

He'll see your undergarments. The panty hose that hold you in like a sausage casing. The bra with the padding beneath to help keep your postbirth breasts from sagging. The stretch marks that pregnancy left behind.

She tried to step away.

"No, don't."

She said, "But I can't."

"Yes, you can."

The dress dropped around her ankles. She closed her eyes in shame. He pressed up against the back of her, his hands coming around the front, capturing her breasts, padding and all, and squeezing the tips.

She threw her head back and moaned.

One of those hands dropped, lowering to her belly, and once again she felt the stain of shame. You could bounce a quarter off her belly, the panty hose were so tight, but then he slipped a hand beneath them and she thought, maybe they weren't so tight, and then his fingers found her and she gasped in pleasure.

He pressed against her and his fingers worked magic. "Do you see?" he asked.

No. She didn't see; she only felt. The long length of him against her backside. The heat of him against her skin. The size of him compared to her. And then there was his hand and what his fingers did and she was sud-

denly finding it hard to breathe because he played her
instrument so perfectly.

"Look," he ordered, dipping deep.

She shook her head, moaned again, shuddered. What
he did to her… She couldn't move, much less open her
eyes.

"Look," he said more sternly, withdrawing his fingers, and she knew it was punishment, and so she
opened her eyes. She saw them there, the two of them
so close they looked like one. Against the backdrop
of the bedroom door they were like phantom figures,
barely discernible. But then her eyes adjusted and she
could see herself, hair tousled, body flush, his arms
cradling her full length.

"Do you see how beautiful you are?" He dipped
his fingers down low again. In the mirror the phantom woman's eyes widened. Her cheeks flushed with
color. Her mouth dropped open. "Do you know how
hard it is for me not to toss you on my bed and rip this
pretty bra off of you?"

She shook her head.

"You're beautiful."

His other hand dipped the edge of her bra down. She
saw that. His finger found the tip of her breast, brushing it, teasing it. Her knees grew weak and she began
to breathe in short gasps. He worked her flesh into a
hard nub, flicking it, at one point almost pinching it,
and his other hand, it kept playing her like a maestro.

"Bren."

"You're beautiful," he whispered again.

And something snapped. She tipped her head back,
twisted, her lips connecting with him even though it

meant she lost the delicious joy his fingers roused. She kissed him and her hand found his center.

"Lauren," he gasped.

She dragged her hand up the length of him and kissed him again. She tore her mouth away to look down at the effect she had on him. She'd had enough of looking. She wanted him to *feel*, too.

They ended up on the bed.

She hadn't even realized they'd moved. One minute she kissed him and the next he was on top of her, his tie dangling down between her breasts, and she knew this would be no slow, sexy seduction. They were half crazed for each other and that was okay. She jerked his tie off. He pulled her panty hose down. She lifted her hips and helped him. Next his hands found the front snap of her bra and the elastic band sprang open so that she was completely exposed and he reared back and stared for so long that she felt the sting of insecurity.

"Beautiful."

He leaned down and kissed her belly. She groaned and lifted her hips. Lord, she'd forgotten, she thought, tossing her head to the side. She'd forgotten how good it could feel.

It'd never felt like this with Paul.

And it hadn't. This was as different as sugar was from salt. As chocolate was from chalk. As cookies were from cream. His mouth suckled her, and she knew he'd come eye to eye with the worst of her stretch marks, but he didn't care. He nipped her, his mouth moving lower, and she couldn't believe he would actually go through with it, that he would kiss her there.

"Bren," his name was a scream because he did kiss her there, and she arched to meet him at the same time she cried out his name and her body pulsed and then tightened. He kept teasing the pleasure from her, refusing to let her up when she tried to move, and she felt herself begin to soar.

"Oh, Bren…"

He kept at it and she rode air currents in the sky. Down and up and down and down. Her body tightened and tensed and she moaned his name once again. When he nipped at her, she began to spiral, her whole body tumbling from the sky. When she opened her eyes, it was almost a shock to realize she lay on a bed, with Bren watching her.

"I've never…"

She didn't know what else to say and he didn't seem to mind that she didn't finish the sentence, because he tenderly kissed the insides of her thighs. She felt him shift and he began to move upward, nuzzling the point of her hip next, and she felt it again, the sexual rush of pleasure that made all her nerve endings tingle. He moved up the length of her and she realized he'd shrugged out of his pants. He still wore his shirt, though, and so she worked the buttons free because she wanted him against her, naked.

His gaze met her own, his brown eyes the same color as a grass fire. "I don't have protection."

"It's okay," she said because it was. If he'd had condoms at his fingertips, that would have said something about him that she wouldn't have liked. "I'm on the pill."

And in case he doubted her word, she hooked her legs behind him, drawing him up toward her. By now he'd stripped his pants completely off and she felt the bare deliciousness of his thighs and the smoothness of his skin even though his leg hair was more wiry than her own, but his flesh…it was so warm she gasped.

"Lauren."

Their hands found each other's and he paused at her center. Was he savoring it, too? Did he want it to last forever like she did? She lifted her hips. He entered her slowly and she began to soar once more, but it was a different sort of throbbing this time, the kind that soothed an ache she hadn't even known she'd had. He pushed her deep into the bed and their fingers entwined and she held on for dear life because she'd never had a man kiss her the way Bren did. It was as if he couldn't get enough. As if he wanted to swallow her whole. As if she were his last meal, and all the while he thrust in and out and in and out…

"Bren," she gasped against his lips as she flew once more.

Her hands ended up above her head. Her heels hooked around him. They both began to fly together. Two birds circling each other in the sky, spiraling up and down and around, until, as one, they reached the apex of the sky, where they began to tumble toward earth…together.

A WHILE LATER—was it seconds? Minutes? Hours? Bren didn't know, but a while later he pulled the covers up and tucked her against him and held her close.

"You're going to be sore tomorrow." She felt good up against him. Like an ornate spoon that fit next to him perfectly in a drawer. "I tried to take it easy on you, but I can't seem to control myself."

"It's okay," she mumbled.

"Don't you go to sleep on me now." He nuzzled her hair. "I have more Valentine's fun in store for you."

She shot up suddenly. "Kyle."

"Hey." He pulled her back around, brushed a strand of hair away from her face. "It's okay. He'll survive a night without you."

Her eyes were big and wide. "We've never spent a night apart."

That he couldn't believe. "Not even for a slumber party?"

She shook her head. "He doesn't sleep over at anyone's house. He gets nightmares."

He saw the truth in her eyes, and the truth told him that Kyle hadn't been as unaffected by her marriage as he'd thought. He might have been young when Paul had died, but he'd clearly been old enough.

"He's not at just anyone's house. He's at his uncle's place."

"He'll still freak out."

"I doubt that."

"Then call him."

His words didn't have the calming effect he'd hoped. "Call him and tell him I'm spending the night with you?"

"Well—"

"I can't do that."

Yes, she could. Or maybe not. Damn it. Dating a woman with a kid was more complicated than he'd figured.

"Do you need me to drive you home?"

"No. That's okay."

He cupped her face with his hands, and, yes, it was very definitely becoming a habit. "Sooner or later he's going to have to sleep without you around."

"What do you mean?"

But she pulled away and it stunned him how much he didn't like her doing that. He wanted to hold her. To reassure her. Instead his hands fell back to his sides.

"You graduate this year, yes?"

She nodded, and she could have no way of knowing how adorable he found her sitting there above him, her hair falling around her shoulder, her makeup slightly smudged around her eyes, her lips swollen from his kisses.

"You know how demanding that will be. Crazy-long days. Working nights. Coming home at odd hours."

He knew he'd struck a nerve, and even though he probably shouldn't have lascivious thoughts when they were discussing something so serious, he couldn't help but notice how completely sexy she looked staring down at him like a tousled kitten.

"But that's next year."

He tugged her down toward him. "Stay." He rolled her beneath him. "At least for a little while. You can call Kyle in a little bit, reassure him that you'll be home."

"I don't know."

He kissed her, gently, reminding her of what she'd be missing out on. It took only seconds for her to soften beneath him and he knew he'd won, at least this time around.

What about next time?

He didn't want to think about next time. There was only here and now and kissing the woman he suspected he was falling in love with.

Chapter Sixteen

She hated sneaking out.

It was as if what they'd done was somehow wrong, but she knew if she woke him up, he'd tempt her again, tugging her back and kissing her and making her forget herself. So instead of calling, she'd simply left.

It was just after midnight and it'd taken a half hour for the taxi to arrive, a half hour during which she'd worried Bren would wake up. A half hour during which she'd sat on the edge of the bed, fully dressed, the light from the bathroom still on and illuminating his muscled body.

She'd done it now.

There was no way they'd be able to go back to the way things were before. No way she could keep this from Kyle, too. Not unless she pretended as if nothing had happened, but that seemed somehow wrong. As if what they'd *done* was wrong. It wasn't, and so that begged the question—why did she feel so ashamed?

The flash of headlights splinted shafts of light through a crack in the drapes and she knew her ride was here. She reached a hand to caress the sprinkling of gray at his temples and then change her mind. She was doing him a favor, she told herself. He was sensitive about their age gap. This way nobody would see her leave. Nobody had to know they were together. Well, aside from Mr. and Mrs. Farrell, but who cared about them?

So she left, and as she slid soundlessly from his house and into the waiting taxi, she admitted that she *did* care. She didn't want to be the cause of his embarrassment or discomfort. She wanted him to be happy.

She could fall in love with the man.

She didn't know why she suddenly had to wipe away tears as the taxi drove off. There was no reason she couldn't see him again. They were two consenting adults. He was single and so was she. So who cared?

The taxi turned left and out of the ranching development where Bren lived, its headlights sweeping a sign. *Reelect Sheriff Bren Connelly.*

The white of the letters against a blue backdrop framed by red stood out like a headline in a newspaper. Big and noticeable and she admitted that she knew nothing of Bren's political life. Last night they'd talked about her getting her bachelor of science in nursing and what going back to school had been like. In turn he'd amused her with funny tales of being on the force—but nothing about the stress he must be under knowing it was an election year and pondering what he would do if he didn't win. Did that mean he would have to change jobs? Would he have to go to work for another city? Would he be out of work?

"He's asleep," her brother said when she walked into his massive front foyer. It always reminded her of a ski lodge. Recessed seating area to her left, one that overlooked the front driveway, not that you could see much out the windows this time of night. Granite floors—

the real deal—not the stamped concrete made to look like rock. And the focal point, a cobblestone fireplace next to a sweeping staircase that led upstairs and to the bedrooms.

"I'll carry him down," Jax said.

"No, no. That's okay."

Uh-oh. She recognized the look on her brother's face. Anxious. On edge. The face of a man who needed sleep but wouldn't get any. He'd been that way ever since he'd decided to "take it easy."

"I take it you had a nice night."

She knew what he meant by *a nice night.*

"Very nice."

Jax's brows shot up. He stared at her for a long moment and said, "So that's how it is?"

Why did she feel her cheeks stain with color? She was a grown woman. It was none of his business who she spent the night with. Or half the night, as the case may be, she amended, glancing up the stairs. Kyle hadn't come charging down. She could relax for a moment.

"Thanks for watching Kyle."

"No problem." He crossed his arms in front of him. "Are you seeing him again?"

So they were having *that* conversation. The one where her brother grilled her about her relationship. "I don't know."

"What do you mean, you don't know?"

Gosh, when had her brother taken on the role of surrogate parent? Their own parents were still alive but distant, both geographically and emotionally, so she supposed she shouldn't be surprised. Jax took his role of protector seriously. He always had.

"I thought you *wanted* me to go out with him."

"I do, but I'm surprised by this sudden leap into... something."

She leaned back on her heels. "Jax, we've only been out on one date."

"A date that lasted until—" he glanced at the clock on the entertainment center on a wall before nodding his chin "—nearly one in the morning."

"So?"

"Is it serious?"

"Did Kyle ask for me?"

He shook his head. "He was down at the stables most of the evening. Tuckered him out, and you haven't answered my question. Is it serious?"

She moved forward and she saw it then—the circles under his eyes. The pinched look on his face. The way his fingers flexed and dug into his forearms. "Jax, what's wrong?"

He seemed surprised by her question. "Nothing. Why?"

She knew him well enough to know that was a lie. "Does it bother you that I'm out with someone? You know, after Paul? I know you two were friends."

He snorted. The arms uncrossed. "I couldn't stand the man."

The words rocked her to the point that she almost took a step back to regain her balance. "Excuse me?"

He nodded, then turned, leading her to the living area. Their footfalls were muffled by a cowhide rug. With a sigh and a scrub of his hands over his face, he sat down. "Man, it feels good to finally get that off my chest."

He'd hated her husband? Okay, maybe not hated, but

definitely didn't like, and her brother liked everybody. It was why he'd been so successful at his contracting business. He'd made contacts while in the military. Heads of state. Heads of corporations. Big-time mucky-mucks. They'd all liked him. So had the men he'd gone to war with. He'd been able to convince them to come work for him under special contracts.

"Why didn't you ever tell me?" she asked, taking a seat next to him.

He glanced out the window, its surface so dark it reflected back their images. He stared out that window and she could see the way his face tightened, from the lips that pinched together to the furrow between his brows.

"He was your husband. What was I supposed to do?"

"Tell me," she said simply, reaching out and grabbing his hand.

He pinned her with a stare, one that demanded complete honesty. "Was it as bad as I think it was?"

She tried to withdraw her hand. He wouldn't let her.

"Was it?" he asked again.

She didn't know how to answer. What to say. Her evening with Bren had thrown her, and now this.

She swallowed hard. "Bad enough."

He twitched. "Did he hit you?"

She tried harder to take her hand away, but once again he wouldn't let her. His own grip grew tighter, as if he tried to squeeze an answer out of her.

"Once." Paul had known he'd crossed the line, though. She'd seen it on his face. "I told him if he ever did it again, I would tell you." That was all she'd needed to say. It'd obviously scared him. "Apparently you're a stronger deterrent than the threat of divorce."

"Why *didn't* you divorce him?" He leaned forward, rested his head on his elbows. "Jeez, Lauren. You should have left his ass years ago."

One word. "Kyle."

His head tipped up, and she saw understanding in his eyes, that and sorrow. He was a man used to violence. A man who handled it with calm authority. A man who'd sacrificed so much to protect the things he loved—except her. She could see that in his eyes, too.

"It's okay." She reached out and grabbed his hand again. "We muddled through."

He sat up, inhaled deeply. "I knew it." She could hear the self-recrimination in his voice and see the disgust with himself on his face and it broke her heart. "Every time I came back stateside, you looked less like yourself."

His gaze met hers and she wanted to cry.

"It's not your fault." She was the one who'd picked a total loser for a husband.

"It is in part." He pressed his lips together. "I saw it and I did nothing about it."

"You're doing something for me now." She felt her voice quaver. "This." She squeezed his hand. "I could never have afforded all this—" she motioned with her free hand to his house " — without your help. Kyle has blossomed. Sure, I hate that he wants to ride bulls, but he gets his craving for adrenaline honestly."

It was an attempt at humor, but it somehow fell flat. He didn't smile; his eyes didn't spark. If anything, the sadness in his eyes grew.

"I should have done something sooner."

"Don't beat yourself up over it."

But she could tell nothing she said would change his

mind that he'd done too little, too late. He had ghosts that haunted him. She'd become more and more aware of them the longer she lived at the ranch. She'd had no idea that some of the specters had to do with her.

He said, "I like Bren."

And she felt a rush of emotion because she liked him, too.

"I looked into his background and what I heard was impressive."

"You did a background check on him?"

There it was. The brief flare of amusement. "You bet your ass I did."

She smiled, too. "Well, I guess it's good to know I'm not dating a serial killer."

"He's a good guy. You could be happy with him."

She could be, and so the question was, why wasn't she jumping for joy? He'd rocked her world tonight. Had made her feel more like a sexy, desirable woman than she ever had in her life. Their chemistry had been off the charts. So why did she feel so much like crying?

"I should probably get Kyle in his own bed."

Her brother patted her knee and she stood up, grateful to him for letting the matter drop. Tomorrow she had class, which meant it'd be a long day.

But as she settled Kyle into bed, she wondered if she was doing the right thing. Kyle mumbled something in his sleep and it made her smile. He'd always done that, she thought, pulling the covers up to his shoulder before drawing back to stare down at him. What if things didn't work out with Bren? What if Kyle got hurt? But as soon as she had the thought, she dismissed it. Whatever happened, Bren would never abandon Kyle. He loved her son, and she loved him for it.

She jolted.

Loved?

No, she quickly amended. She didn't "love him" love him. It was way too soon for that, but something had happened tonight. Something remarkable and exhilarating and terrifying. And she found herself thinking, why couldn't she be happy?

Why not indeed.

Chapter Seventeen

She'd left in the middle of the night.

Relax, Bren. She had a kid to get back home to. She had to leave.

Yes, but without saying goodbye? He'd like to think what they'd shared was more than a quick fling followed by an even faster retreat.

"So just be alert and stay vigilant," Bren said to a room full of deputies. "It's not likely that the annual Via Del Caballo President's Day Parade will be the target of a terrorist attack, but these days you never know. At this time we remain low on the threat-level list."

There were nods around the room and Bren said, "That's it. Stay safe. I'll do another briefing before the parade on Friday."

His deputies stood. He closed his briefing binder with a snap. He would miss this if he didn't win re-election. Of course, there was always the chance he could go to work for another law enforcement agency, but these were his deputies and he'd grown close to them in the eight years he'd been their sheriff.

"So I hear you had a good time the other night."

Bren turned toward the man who'd spoken, Chris Carson, one of his first supporters and a good friend.

"Oh, yeah? Who'd you hear that from?" He came around the podium, one hand clutching the binder, his other moving to his right hip.

"Frank Farrell wouldn't shut up about the hot little number you had on your arm."

Bren hoped he concealed his dismay. "When was that?"

"At the coffee shop this morning." Chris's bright blue eyes glowed with amusement. "I got the feeling she must be something else to look at if it had old Frank up in arms."

Bren didn't know what to say. It was clear Chris didn't know about the age gap between him and Lauren. And he doubted Frank would make a big deal over it. It was probably more that she'd been dressed like a sexy siren than that there was a difference in their ages. But the fact that Frank was talking about him was disconcerting.

"What'd he say, exactly?"

"Just that you'd taken to cradle-robbing, which made me think she must be really hot. Frank's wife is about as good-looking as a cube of ice. I don't think that man's had sex for decades."

The twinkle in Chris's eyes only increased as Bren tried to contain his consternation. Clearly his friend found his discomfort amusing.

Okay. Get ahold of yourself. It's probably nothing. Nobody's going to listen to windbag Frank.

So he worked hard to get the dismay off his face. He even managed to shrug and it felt good because it loosened his tense shoulders. "I took that little boy's mom out for Valentine's Day," he said. "You know, the one I've been teaching to ride."

Chris nodded. "Hope she showed you a little gratitude afterward."

He bristled. He didn't know why. Chris was just having some fun at his expense, but he didn't like anyone thinking of Lauren that way. She was so much more than a quick fling.

So much more?

He straightened. "Frank Farrell is a jerk not fit to lick Lauren Danners's boots. Next time you see him, tell him to butt out of my business."

Chris's eyes had widened, parallel wrinkles forming between them. "Sorry, bud. I didn't mean to step on toes."

Bren forced himself to relax again. If Frank was blabbing his mouth all over town, it could have only one purpose. He was trying to cause trouble over the reelection. Wouldn't work, though. He'd make sure of that.

"Don't worry about it." He clapped the man on his shoulder. "I just don't like men like Frank passing judgment on someone like Lauren. She deserves better."

"Got it." Chris gave him a salute, his gold star twinkling nearly as bright as his eyes. "Never liked Frank anyway."

In that they were in perfect agreement. "Stay safe," he said.

His friend nodded. "You, too." Although he had a better chance of that than Chris. These days he lived his life behind a desk.

"You bringing her to the parade on Saturday?"

"Actually, I'm in it."

"Oh, yeah?" Chris asked as he walked back to his office near the front of the Via Del Caballo sheriff's department. "Are you the grand marshal?"

"Nothing so grandiose." He shook his head. "Andrew and the boys thought it would be good for me to be in it. You know, shake some hands, kiss some babies."

"Ah, the tough life of a public official."

Yeah. But for how much longer?

HE'D TEXTED HER while she was in class. She'd heard her backpack vibrate and, yes, smiled when she'd read the message.

See you tomorrow?

Tomorrow, not tonight?

She quickly contained her disappointment. At least he wasn't rushing her. Besides, she needed to swing by that nursing home tonight and put in an application. It wasn't the job she wanted, but it would pay the bills. Time to get serious about finding a job.

And so she'd quickly typed the word yes.

But it wasn't until later that evening that she learned Bren had scheduled a jumping lesson for her son, something she wasn't particularly thrilled about, but that she'd known had been coming. That's what "seeing her tomorrow" was all about. She tried not to read too much into it, focusing instead on how much she appreciated Bren's help. Kyle had healed quickly after being stepped on and he couldn't wait to get back at it, especially since they'd learned he hadn't won a buckle at the rodeo where he'd gotten hurt. Someone else had come along and scored higher in the main performance. A couple someones, actually. It'd lit a fire in Kyle's eyes and he'd become determined to ride even better at his next rodeo in a few weeks, calling Bren up and arranging the lesson.

Bren hadn't asked to take her out again.

You're overthinking things, said the little voice.

She expected him to call that night, and when he didn't, she ignored the burning in the pit of her stomach.

So what? said that same voice. *You're a big girl. You can text him.*

And so she did, taking the bull by the horns and texting, Miss you.

It was a full forty-five excruciating minutes later when she received a miss you, too back.

Dear goodness, she had it bad. The next night she had the same thought when her stomach fluttered as she drove home. Everyone was at the stables, and when she saw Bren's big black law enforcement truck, she gripped the steering wheel just a little too tight. They were in that in-between point, she told herself, where she wasn't sure what to do when she first saw him. Did she rush up to him and kiss him? Give him a big hug? Act as if nothing had happened? The uncertainty caused her palms to sweat.

"She's here!"

The announcement came from inside the arena, even though she could make out nothing through the glass panels that lined the wide side of the arena. Her heart began to race as if she were a runner at the starting line when she walked toward the wide door. She paused just inside to get her bearings. Her son sat on Rowdy in the smallest saddle she'd ever seen, a bridle with a flimsy-looking bit in Rowdy's mouth. From somewhere, Lauren didn't know where, her brother had found some horse jumps, or probably more accurately, purchased them.

And there were two people who stood in the middle of the arena: Bren—instantly recognizable in his blue jeans and black hat—and a woman she didn't recognize.

"Mom, watch."

She waited for Bren to look her way and acknowledge her, and when he did, Lauren experienced a kind of post-reactive jolt, an instant remembrance of what it'd been like to be held by him, kissed by him, touched by him.

Only who was that woman?

"Mom," her son called.

"Look at the fence," the woman called out, following her son's progress around the arena.

Lauren jerked her gaze away from the man she'd spent an incredible night with, just in time to see what Kyle was about to do.

Jump.

"Kyle—"

"It's okay, Mama," Jax said, coming up to stand behind her on the rail. "Natalie's got it covered."

Natalie? Who the devil was Natalie? And why hadn't Bren smiled at her?

She told herself that he was busy. She told herself that he was focusing on her son. She told herself a million things, none of which she believed, because she'd seen something in his eyes, something that scared her as much as watching Kyle gallop toward two crossed rails, her heart racing. Forty feet. Thirty feet. Twenty. She resisted the urge to close her eyes as Kyle leaned forward and Rowdy took off.

They sailed over the jump.

Lauren didn't realize she held the wooden rail too

tight until she felt the pain beneath her nails. She forced herself to let it go as her son let out a whoop of delight.

"Natalie says this will really help his balance." Her brother nodded with his chin toward where Natalie stood. "I guess she's been working with several of Bren's students."

Why wouldn't he look at her? Who was this Natalie? She wanted to scream. Instead she pasted what she hoped was a composed smile on her face and said, "That's great," even though she didn't feel great at all.

"Can I do it again?" Kyle asked.

The woman shook her head. "No. Rowdy is getting tired. We should take it easy on him."

Kyle's whole body slumped in the saddle, but he immediately turned Rowdy toward her. "I'm going to do it again next week."

Of course he was. With the beautiful Natalie. She couldn't wait.

"Hi," said the woman with a big smile that only made her blue eyes seem like twin jewels. "I don't believe we've met. I'm Natalie Reynolds."

And Lauren immediately felt like an idiot. Reynolds. Chance Reynolds's wife. Of course that's who it was. She'd heard all about the woman from Kyle one night.

"I'm Lauren," she said, her gaze sliding past the woman's long blond hair and landing on Bren, who'd followed her over. She smiled at the man. He smiled back, but it was a small grin and everything inside her turned inside out because she'd envisioned their first meeting after, well, going differently.

"Hey," she said to him softly.

"Hey," was all he said back.

What was going on? Was he mad at her for sneaking out of the house? Was that it? And why did his cool greeting stab her in the heart? It wasn't like they'd professed their love for each other.

"You've got a good horse in Rowdy." Natalie smiled at her brother. "He should be perfect for your program."

"I sure hope so, since Brielle is arriving next weekend."

His new hippotherapist. Everything was new around here, including the way it felt to have Bren act as if nothing had happened between them. She'd expected a hug. Maybe even a kiss. Certainly no less than a smile. She would have to apologize. Clearly her sneaking out had upset him.

"Will you help me put him away, Uncle Jax?"

She saw her brother's eyes light up. Her son was good for him. After their conversation the other night, she was sure of it.

"I'll help." Natalie smiled at her one last time before letting herself out through the wide gate set into the rail. They all three disappeared into a grooming stall.

Lauren had shifted her gaze to Bren, watching him, waiting for him to look in her direction again. "Look, about the other night." She swallowed, even though it felt like she had a mouth full of sand. "I didn't mean to upset you by sneaking out."

"You didn't," he said, walking toward her. She tensed. He stopped in front of her. She couldn't breathe all of a sudden. She saw him glance behind her, no doubt making sure the coast was clear, before leaning down and kissing her and she thought, *Everything's all right.* He just wasn't advertising their relationship to everyone. That was okay, she assured herself, closing her eyes and kissing him back. He probably didn't know Jax already knew. Then the kiss heated up and all was right in her world.

He pulled back far too soon. "God, I've missed you," he said softly.

She wanted to laugh like a child. To howl at the moon. To do a little jig. "Me, too."

"Why didn't you come over last night?"

He'd wanted her to come over? Then what was the "see you tomorrow" text all about? She wanted to ask him that very question, but she could hear footsteps behind her as Bren took a step back and she realized he really was trying to act as if there were nothing between them in front of her brother. She turned, only it wasn't her brother. It was Natalie.

"I've got to get back home."

Bren smiled at Natalie and little pinpoints of jealousy punctured Lauren's heart. "Short drive."

"I know," Natalie said. "It's nice." She caught her gaze. "Tell your brother this place is amazing."

"Thanks." She smiled back because there was something instantly likable about the woman in front of her. She'd heard she was some kind of big deal in the horse-show world. "Although he hears it all the time."

"I'm sure he does."

They were alone again. "It's okay," she told Bren. "Jax knows about what happened the other night."

"Yes, but Natalie doesn't."

And that mattered to him? The pinpricks widened. "Did you want our…" crap, what to call it? "…relationship to be a secret?"

She hated the way her question had sounded. Surprised. Accusatory. Maybe even a little bit angry.

"No. I mean, yes." He glanced back toward the

grooming stall. "Look, one of my deputies told me the other day that Frank Farrell was spouting his mouth off about our date."

It took her a moment to place who Frank Farrell was, and when she did, couldn't help but snap out, "So?"

"I just don't want people to talk."

Because of his election. She got it then, felt a little less offended, but if she were honest, only a little.

"I'm glad your brother knows," he said, closing the distance between them again, bending down, his eyes sparking when they focused on her lips. "I really wanted to run over and kiss you."

Okay, so maybe that took the sting out of his words. But he still could have called her last night. Asked her to come over. That he didn't left her feeling troubled.

You need to relax.

And perhaps she did, she told the ever-present voice. She was new to dating again. New to this feeling of abject terror. As though she was about to do something wrong.

"There's a parade this weekend." Bren was all smiles again as he stared into her eyes. "You and Kyle should come."

This weekend? What about tonight? Why couldn't she come over after he was done here? She could even sneak over later...

Wait.

Sneak over? What was she thinking? Where was her pride? If he wanted to see her, he should ask.

"That sounds good."

And still she waited for it. Waited for him to invite her over again. To ask her to dinner tonight.

"Great. Then I'll see you this weekend."

Her brother had come out then, leading the horse. Bren smiled and walked toward him, leaving her there on the rail, the sting of humiliation coloring her cheeks.

You're reading too much into this.

Was she? she wondered. Or was she reading the situation exactly right?

Chapter Eighteen

It was the longest week of Bren's life. On Thursday they'd had a homicide, and in the small town of Via Del Caballo, that put everyone in a tailspin. Work was work, however, and when push came to shove, he did all the shoving. So he'd missed out on seeing Lauren, forced, instead, to ponder his memories of their time together. In some ways that was worse. The physical effects of his memories were damn near embarrassing.

He thought about their conversations over the past few weeks, too. Strangely, that's what he missed the most. He and Lauren could talk, really talk, but there hadn't even been time for that and he knew she must be thinking he was giving her the brush-off. So he'd sent her flowers and a note that he hoped to see her at the parade.

He just didn't know if she'd show. She hadn't called him. Hadn't texted him thanks. He'd heard nothing.

And so he sat waiting in the pre-parade lineup, leaning against a fancy red-and-white sports car they'd rented for the occasion, waiting for things to get rolling, which should happen any moment now. It wasn't like, as an elected official, he'd be riding in a car that would be judged by parade officials, but he still had to

line up early. They'd decorated the convertible with Reelect Sheriff Connelly signs. His job would be to sit in
the backseat and wave. In the distance, one of the high
school bands played a melody that was just the tiniest
bit off-key. Someone blared music, a float up ahead of
him, one decked out in so much red, white and blue
it looked like a political party had sacrificed all their
leftover convention decorations in the name of patriot-
ism. By his watch, they had five, maybe ten minutes
before things would get going, and with each minute
that passed, he wondered…would she show?

"At least it's a nice day and not nine hundred de-
grees outside," said his campaign consultant and the
man playing chauffeur today, Jerry Blaylock. "Nothing worse than being forced to sit out in the sun waiting for a parade to start."

Jerry should know. He'd helped out with his cam-
paigns from the start, the older man a full-time consultant for various elected officials throughout the state
of California. Bren considered himself lucky to secure
his services.

"These are the days I'm glad I wear a cowboy—"

"Bren!"

His words died a quick death. His heart leaped. His
body jolted with what felt like ten thousand volts of
energy.

He turned, and there she was, Kyle by her side, and
just like the other day, his gut kicked at the sight of her.
She wore pigtails again, damn it. And she looked so gorgeous and so alluring in a white linen dress that hung
off her shoulders that he felt her sexiness like a kick in
the groin. She paired the outfit with cowboy boots and

as she walked through the crowd, she drew the attention of every male in the vicinity.

Kyle flung himself into his arms. Bren pulled his eyes away from Lauren but only with a herculean effort. The little boy had wrapped his arms around him, his head buried in his chest.

"Hey," he said softly, some other emotion filling his soul. "How you been?"

Kyle reared back, pinned him with an accusatory stare. "Where have you been?"

That was one thing about kids. They always said exactly what was on their minds. "I had to work this week." And he added for Lauren's benefit, "We had a homicide."

He looked up from beneath the brim of his cowboy hat.

It hit him then, right then, that he was falling in love with her

"You mean somebody died?"

Once again it took every ounce of his willpower to look away. "Sadly, yes."

"Who?"

"Don't know yet. That's why we've been working so hard."

Kyle nodded as if the excuse met with his approval. Bren had had to cancel his lesson with him this week, but if he'd known how much those lessons meant to Kyle, he wouldn't have done it.

"Hi," he said to Lauren as Kyle stepped back.

"Hello."

That voice. He'd never noticed before how throaty and sexy it was and just how plain perfect he found it. He threw in the towel then. A part of him had convinced himself he could keep his distance. He'd thought he could cool it a little. He'd been kidding himself, and so he reached for her hand, her eyes widening at the contact, but they snapped open even more when he pulled her to him.

"Get the flowers?" he asked.

"Yes."

"Good." And then he kissed her. Hard.

Kyle gasped. He thought Lauren might have, too. All it took was for their lips to collide and Bren forgot where they stood, and the people that walked by, and that he was soon to be on public display and so should probably be on his best behavior. He didn't care about any of it.

He drew back, but only because Kyle said, "Jeez, you guys," which made him look down and smile.

"Sorry, buddy. I've missed your mom."

His young student stared between the two of them, and it was clear he'd had no clue he and Lauren had become an item. He would have expected the kid to be thrilled; instead he studied them as if he didn't know what to think.

"I take it this was your date on Valentine's Day?"

Jerry. He'd completely forgotten about the man who'd been standing nearby.

"Ah, actually...yes." He turned to the gray-haired man. "This is Lauren."

He'd never thought of Jerry as being particularly judgmental. He saw in an instant he'd missed the character flaw. Jerry eyed Lauren up and down and it was clear what he thought of her, and it wasn't flattering.

"Lauren, this is Jerry. He's my campaign consultant."

She still seemed a little dazed, her lips swollen from

his kiss, the hand she held out to Jerry visibly shaking. "Nice to meet you."

Jerry took it, the smile he gave her a tinge on the sleazy creepy-politician side, and it made Bren immediately bristle, to the point that he said, "Lauren's in the RN program at Santa Barbara State. She graduates later this year."

The words had the desired effect. Jerry even drew back a bit, like a dog that'd been growled at by a smaller dog. Or maybe it was the tone he'd used when he'd said the words that had Jerry looking that way, but he wiped his face clean of expression, a talent that Bren sometimes wished he had.

"Wow," Jerry said. "Impressive."

"She has a 4.0 GPA, too," Kyle said.

Bren doubted Kyle even knew what a GPA was, much less what it meant, but it was clear even the little boy had picked up on Jerry's veiled disapproval.

"She's going to graduate honorably next fall."

Bren had to bite back a smile. "You mean with honors, buddy."

"And I won't graduate until the end of the fall semester, almost a year from now," Lauren added.

"Wow," Jerry said again, but he couldn't keep his eyes from sweeping Lauren up and down, and for the first time since working with the man, Bren wanted to knock his teeth in. "You're a lucky man, Bren."

Just then someone blew a whistle and Bren looked toward the front of the parade. One of the horse units had started to move, hooves clopping on the pavement. The marching band suddenly improved tenfold.

"Well," Lauren said, having followed his gaze. "We should probably find a spot to watch."

He turned toward the fancy sports car. "You could have a front-row seat in my car."

"What?" Jerry said at the same time Kyle shouted, *"Cool!"* his early disgruntlement having obviously died a quick death in the wake of his desire to ride in the red Mustang.

"I don't know," Lauren said.

He wouldn't give her a choice, he admitted, not even if it meant enlisting Kyle's help in convincing her. "I'm not taking no for an answer."

"Let's go, Mom."

It was clear she was torn. It was equally clear she didn't want to disappoint her son. And just like she always did, she put his needs above her desires. It was one of the things he most admired about her.

"Well, if you're sure it's okay." She eyed Jerry.

His campaign consultant lifted his hands. "Not up to me."

Because if it were up to Jerry, he wouldn't let her ride along. Well, it wasn't up to Jerry, and so he turned and opened the sports car's door.

"After you, m'lady."

For the first time she smiled. A real smile. Not the fake one she'd just given him when she first walked up or the forced one she'd used later. It set her eyes aglow and made him remember things from their night together that he probably shouldn't be thinking about.

Kyle jumped into the backseat ahead of her. She followed behind, but Bren stopped her. "Sit up on top."

She looked confused.

"Like this?" Kyle sat on the fold-down roof.

"Exactly like that."

"Are you sure about this?" she asked as she took a seat next to her son.

"I've never been more sure about something in my life."

KYLE COULDN'T STOP talking the whole time they drove the giant circle of the parade. Somewhere in between First and Third Streets he'd lost his dismay at spotting his mom kissing his steer-riding coach, but she'd seen the look on her son's face and it surprised her. She knew Kyle adored Bren, but clearly the idea of his dating his mother was strange.

Perhaps too strange.

"Did you have fun?" Bren asked her son.

Kyle nodded. "I saw a bunch of people from my school. They're going to be so jealous."

"And how about you?"

She shelved her concerns for a moment. "It was great."

His campaign manager had faded away, thank goodness. She didn't like the man. Not at all.

"Just great?"

Damn his smile and the teasing glint in his eyes. She'd wanted to be mad at him, had been determined to give him a cold shoulder despite the flowers he'd sent her yesterday. How hard would it have been to pick up the phone and call her during the week? He hadn't. And, yes, she'd been hurt. But now here he was, smiling at her, inviting her to ride in a parade with him, and she could feel herself falling again.

Falling, taunted that little voice.

Maybe not that. Or maybe it *was* that. She didn't know, because she couldn't concentrate when he was around.

"It was fun," she amended.

He leaned down next to her, and every nerve ending in her body erupted as he whispered in her ear, "I know a better way to have fun."

She blushed, glanced down at Kyle, but her son was too busy trying to peek under the hood of the sports car to pay attention to them.

"Why didn't you call me this week?"

She hadn't meant to blurt the words, but suddenly she didn't care that it wasn't the right moment to confront him. She'd seen him that one night, and then...nothing.

He looked away for a second and she saw in his eyes that she'd made him uncomfortable with her question. She gleaned her own answer then, and she didn't like it. He'd been trying to avoid her. But then why the flowers?

"I thought maybe it might be easier if we took things a little more slow."

She pinned him with a stare. "Easier for whom?"

He had the grace to look ashamed. "I realized quickly that it was the wrong call." He faced her fully. "I want to see you. As much as possible. If that's all right with you."

She could read the earnestness in his eyes and the genuine remorse for hurting her.

"Don't do that again."

He nodded. "I won't. I promise." He lightly cupped her face with his palms, the gesture so tender and so familiar that she felt tears fill her eyes.

"It made me think you didn't want to see me anymore," she added.

"Never."

He kissed her then and she gave herself up to it, only this kiss was unlike any she'd ever experienced before. It was at once tender and passionate. Both soft and rough. Both perfect and imperfect because she wanted it to go on forever and she knew it couldn't given where they were.

"We should get going."

The words came from a distance and it was only when Bren drew back that she realized they came from her son. "Uncle Jax is expecting us for lunch."

He was. They were supposed to meet at Ed's Eatery, and an invitation to join them was on the tip of Lauren's tongue, but something stopped her.

Kyle.

She could tell he wasn't sure what to think of Bren's new status as her boyfriend.

Is that what he is? she asked herself.

Yes, she admitted. Or that's what she wanted him to be. The realization was both exhilarating and terrifying at the same time. She hadn't expected Kyle to react the way he had, though, and so she forced herself to step out of his arms.

"You're right. We probably should get going."

She had a feeling Bren knew what was going on. He didn't seem to take it personally that she was running off to have lunch without him.

"See you later tonight?" he asked in a voice so low she knew it was for her ears only.

"Yes."

He smiled as he turned and walked away. She smiled, too.

Chapter Nineteen

She spent the night at Bren's house. Lauren had never felt more naughty in her life. She'd had to sneak out of her apartment like a misbehaving teenager. She'd left Kyle with Jax, who was watching TV in her family room, her brother not above teasing her as she dashed toward the door. The teasing she could handle, but she'd fretted the whole way over to Bren's place that she was doing the right thing.

"You made it?"

She was so instantly struck by his standing there, all five o'clock shadow and sexy cowboy, that she couldn't even smile at him.

"I'm here."

He reached for her. She sank into his arms. It took one kiss for him to convince her that she should have come over sooner. She needed this thing with Bren, whatever it was. Afterward he held her and they talked. She confessed that she'd spent the first year after Paul's death beating herself up because there'd been a part of her that had wanted the marriage to end, no matter how it happened. He confessed that he'd never been serious about a woman in his life, until her. They ended up making love again, only this time it was a coupling that brought tears to both their eyes.

She kept her evening jaunts from Kyle. Bren resumed his role as coach. Her son seemed much happier with Bren in that role. He took to watching them with an eagle eye, something that kept them both on edge. They'd never really talked about keeping their relationship a secret from her son, but that's what they ended up doing.

Until the photo appeared online.

She hadn't even known about it, and if she had, she probably wouldn't have had the first clue about how to find it. Leave it to her ten-year-old son to know everything there was to know about the internet and to bring it to her attention first.

"They're making fun of you and Bren online."

She'd been in the midst of studying for an important test, and so at first she misheard him. "Who's making fun of you?"

"No," Kyle said in the way that kids had of speaking to adults like they were stupid. "Not *me*. You and Bren."

She about dropped the paper she'd been studying. Kyle sat at the kitchen table, the windows that overlooked the backyard dark, and so she could see the panicked look on her own face as she came around behind him.

Bren held a woman close, the look on his face one of sexy male satisfaction, the woman he held staring up at him like she wanted to push him against the rear of the car next to where they stood and have her wicked way with him. A red car. A white dress. That was *her*. The day of the parade, right after he'd kissed her. The caption read "Via Del Caballo's finest."

She glanced down at Kyle. Her heart was beating a million miles per hour, and she could tell her son was troubled by the photo. He glanced up at her, his brown eyes full of…what? Was it consternation or distress?

"You look…"

She waited for him to finish the sentence. To add the word *pretty* or *funny* or even *stupid*. She would have taken anything in that moment, but he clearly didn't want to say what was on his mind for fear of hurting her.

"I look good," she finished for him because she did. Even though the dress had been conservative, it set her figure off to advantage. The shoulders had slipped down, exposing a bare expanse of skin. You couldn't see the bottom of that dress. Or tell that it was loose and down to her knees. The photo had cut that off so that all you saw was bare skin and her hanging all over Bren, one of her pigtails flipped back over a shoulder and making her look about fifteen years old.

Her eye caught on some of the comments.

What is she, ten?

I didn't know Via Del Caballo had hookers.

Looks like Sheriff Connelly was making an arrest.

And the worst: *I'd like to spread her—*

She slammed the lid of Kyle's laptop closed.

"Hey." For the first time ever, she saw something else in Kyle's eyes, something that made her stomach turn over. Anger. And also disgust. Maybe even dismay.

"Hey. What's that look for?"

Kyle peered up at her with as studious an expression as she'd ever seen. "They're calling you a slut, Mom."

"Well, I'm not."

"But that's what they're saying."

"They're just internet bullies, Kyle. You have to ignore them."

He tipped his chin up, and he looked just like Jax in that moment, so much so that her heart lurched into her throat. She wanted to reach out and stroke his baby-smooth cheek, but she knew if she did that, he'd only jerk away.

"It's just one photo." No big deal, she told herself.

"The kids at school have seen it."

"What?"

He nodded. "That's how I found the picture. One of the kids at school showed it to me. Asked me if it was you."

"And what'd you tell them?"

"I told them you and Bren were dating."

And the kids had been cruel. She could see it in his expression. She didn't want to know what they'd said. She doubted it had anything to do with "dating." Probably more like...

"Goody," she said. "That ought to shut them up."

Kyle just nodded. Bless her son's heart. The anger and disappointment had faded into righteous indignation. "They were being mean."

"Kids can be cruel sometimes." She took a deep breath. "Don't let them get you down."

But it bothered her. She hated that Kyle had to learn about the internet in such a way and how people could turn something so innocent into something lewd and tawdry. She hadn't even noted what site it was on. Tumblr? Instagram? Facebook? Did it really matter? The damage was done.

"I hear you sneak out at night."

She sank into a nearby chair, the blood having drained from her face. "You do?"

He nodded. "I hear Uncle Jax come in." He pinned her with a stare. "I know what you've been up to."

For the first time in her life, Lauren felt like a bad mom. She closed her eyes, tried to calm herself, tried to think what to say. In the end she decided on the truth.

"I thought you might be bothered that I was seeing him."

When she opened her eyes, her son stared at her with a look reminiscent of someone twice his age. "I was."

She swallowed. "And are you still?"

He shook his head. "You're a good mom. You deserve to be happy."

Her eyes burned. She had to take another deep breath to keep from losing it there and then.

"Thanks, kiddo," she choked out.

"But this is going to get Bren in trouble."

"No, it's not." She shook her head firmly. "It's just a photo on Facebook. It'll be at the bottom of the feed before tomorrow night."

"It's in the paper, Mom."

She jerked upright. "What?"

"That's where the kid at school found it. Some society page or something. You and Bren were center stage."

"WHAT ARE WE going to do?"

Bren stared down at the photo in question and it seemed like his stomach turned inside out.

"It's no big deal," he said.

"It's in the paper."

And he knew exactly who'd taken it. Miriam Webber. She took pictures for the community page, and she was best friends with Frank Farrell.

Damn it. How had he missed that? How had Jerry missed it?

But he couldn't blame his campaign consultant.

This was all on his own shoulders. He'd known people were watching. He just hadn't cared.

"Kyle's being teased at school about it."

His chin snapped up. "What?"

She nodded. "He didn't complain about it outright, but I know it bothers him. And do you blame him? The paper allows comments on the pictures. Did you read what people were saying?"

His stomach flipped again, but if there was one thing being in the military had taught him, it was that panic didn't do anybody any good.

"We'll handle it." He went over to her. She stood at his kitchen window, and if the people commenting on that photo could see her now, they'd know she wasn't some kind of floozy. They'd see a distressed single mom. Someone who cared deeply about her son. "It's okay."

He clasped her shoulders. He was about to bend down and give her a kiss but she said, "He knows I've been sneaking out."

That stopped him cold. They'd talked about how she was keeping her relationship with him away from Kyle. He hadn't liked it, but he understood her reasoning.

"He was pissed," she said.

"He doesn't like me?"

Her gaze snapped to his. "No. That's not it at all. He was mad because I didn't trust him with the truth. He didn't say it, but I could see it in his eyes." She looked away. "It was the first time I've ever felt ashamed as a parent."

He tipped her chin up, and his heart broke at the sadness in her gaze. "Don't beat yourself up."

Her eyes changed color with her mood, he'd noticed. They were hazel when she was happy and laughing. They were dark brown when she was sleepy or filled with passion. They were a rusty brown when she was uptight or felt strongly about something.

"My first time dating someone and I'm mucking it all up," she said, her gaze darting around his face as if she sought clues in the way he stared down at her.

"You're not mucking it up." He rested his hands on her shoulders, staring at her reflection in the surface of the glass. "It might be messy. We might make mistakes at times, but we're a couple."

She turned to face him. "Do you love me, Bren?"

The words knocked the stuffing out of him. Love? Was that was this was? Was that why it felt like he couldn't breathe every time he opened up his front door and she stood there? Why no matter what his mood, when he kissed her, she made him smile. Why he couldn't think about anything else but her. He could be having the worst day of his life, and being town sheriff, there were some pretty dark moments, but when he picked up the phone and it was her on the other end, it always brightened his day.

So he took a deep breath, did what he always did whenever she stared up at him so intently—he cupped her face, tenderly, almost reverently, and said the words that had been building in his heart.

"I do."

He saw her eyes widen just a bit. But then they filled

with tears. She tried to look away, but he wouldn't let her, the brown in her eyes suddenly tinged by a luminous green.

"Do you love me?" he asked.

She began to nod, slowly at first and then faster and faster, and suddenly he was pulling her into his arms. She let him hold her, but only for a moment. Then he felt her stiffen and he didn't want to hear what was coming next. Like a sailor that sensed an impending storm, he knew rough seas were ahead.

"I love you enough to walk away while you deal with reelection."

He shook his head emphatically. "That's ridiculous. We can weather this storm. It's just a stupid picture."

"That might influence voters."

"It's not like that. I'm not some high-profile congressman. I'm the town sheriff. No one will care."

"You haven't read the comments."

"I don't need to." He rubbed her shoulders. "It's okay."

She shook her head again. "It's not just the picture. It's what it's putting Kyle through, too." The tears were back. "He didn't say anything, but I know he must have been teased pretty bad. He was bullied in the school before. It's one of the reasons why we left. I don't want that to start back up again."

"So marry me."

"What?"

"Marry me," he said, and after he said the words, he knew he'd never been so certain about something in his life. "That'll take all the wind out of their sails."

She blinked up at him. "You're crazy."

He smiled. "In love."

He kissed her and once again he felt her soften in his arms, but it was short-lived because she pulled back. He could read the resolve on her face.

"I'm not marrying you."

For the first time he felt a pang of concern. "Why not?"

"First of all, I have a son to think about. I can't just spring something like this on him. It wouldn't be fair."

"Kyle would be thrilled."

"Would he?"

He thought back to the way Kyle had looked when he'd kissed his mom and he wasn't so sure. Lauren pounced on that uncertainty.

"He's ten. Four years ago he lost his dad. He's in a strange new town with a bunch of kids he doesn't know and they're teasing him about a picture of his mom and the town sheriff. Add in a shotgun wedding and the rumors will fly."

"So what?"

She jerked back then. "So what? Do you not care that this is our life we're talking about?"

"So what if I lose the election? I'll live."

She threw her shoulders back and her eyes were spitting fire. "I will not be responsible for the loss of your position as town sheriff."

"So what are you saying? You want to break up with me?"

No. She didn't want that. He could see it in her eyes, and it almost made him pull her toward him again. Almost.

"Bren, we have to be smart about this. I'm bad for you right now."

"You're twelve years younger than me." He all but shouted the words. *"Big deal."*

"To some people in this town it is a big deal. Clearly. And your opponent is clearly going to make it a big deal."

"Hank? Hank Cresta couldn't care less about me. It's that damn Frank Farrell that will make the fuss."

"So you agree I'm a problem."

"No." He ran a hand through his hair. "That's not what I meant. It's just, it's not Hank who would make waves. It's Frank."

"Why?"

He hesitated to share the story.

"Bren, what aren't you telling me?"

He shook his head. "It's nothing. Or it was nothing. I dated the man's daughter back in high school. She made it clear she wanted a commitment, but we were seventeen, for heaven's sake. I was riding bulls and having fun. I didn't want to be tied down."

"You broke his daughter's heart."

"That was decades ago. The woman's moved on. She's married now and has three kids."

"But he'll never forgive you for breaking his little girl's heart."

He winced. He'd never really wanted to believe that was the root of Frank's problem with him, but when she said it like that, he supposed it was.

"And you think he's going to just waltz away from that photo without saying a word." She stared at him like he'd lost his mind.

"Yeah." He hoped he would. He *assumed* he would. What good would it do for Frank to stir the pot?

"You're kidding yourself."

"So you'd just walk away?"

She stared up at him and it was one of those moments

when he knew what she wanted, and it had nothing to do with leaving him. Right then he read her desire to stay by his side, but she'd made up her mind that that would be a bad idea, and he knew her well enough to know that once she made up her mind to do something, she did it. It was one of the many things he loved about her.

"It's just temporary," she said softly.

"Will it be?"

She nodded. "After the election, if we still have feelings for each other…"

He had to work to keep his voice even. "Of course I'll have feelings for you."

She lifted her chin even higher. "Then we'll be okay."

No. They wouldn't be okay. He didn't want to give her up. Not now. Not ever.

"Lauren—"

"No." She held up a hand when he started to move toward her. "Don't do it. Don't cup my face with your hands. If you do that, I'll never be able to walk out of here."

Damn it.

Tears had started to form in her eyes. "We have to do this, Bren. *I* have to for my son's sake. He deserves better than the teasing and ribbing that will come from my dating you. I have to for *your* sake because you deserve to be reelected." Her voice had started to shake and he knew she wanted to cry. "You're a good man, Sheriff Connelly. I could never forgive myself if I crushed your future. We have to because if this is the real deal, we'll pick up the pieces in June when the election is over and Kyle is out of school."

He knew he fought a losing battle. What's more, he knew she was right.

"So this is goodbye?"

She lifted her chin. "For now."

Damn it, he felt his own eyes begin to burn, and he never cried. "Can I kiss you goodbye?"

He thought she would say no. Another tear fell. She wiped it away with a hand that shook. "Sure," she said with a voice gone tight with tears.

He moved in close to her, slowly, like she was a filly he might startle away. He almost cupped her face, but he stopped himself just in time. Instead he bent down and touched his lips to hers, lightly at first but then with more and more pressure. He couldn't seem to stop himself. He drank of her like a man who'd never tasted water. Like a sailor coming in from a long trip at sea. Like a man who feared he'd never taste something so sweet again.

She broke the kiss. His arms dropped back to his sides.

"Goodbye, Bren."

And then she was gone.

Chapter Twenty

It was the right thing to do. Lauren wasn't thinking of herself. She was thinking of him.

"Mom?" Kyle said as she walked through the door. She'd left him alone while she ran over to Bren's. She could now add child endangerment to her list of sins.

"What's wrong?" he asked.

"Nothing."

He slowly stood up. He'd been sitting in the same chair she'd left him in earlier, when he'd shown her that photo. "Did you break up with Bren?"

She'd told herself that Kyle didn't need to know what had happened. She'd had it all worked out in her head—what she would say to him. How she would act. But the look of sympathetic understanding on her son's face was her undoing.

Bless you, Paul, for giving me such a child.

She let the past go in that moment. All the hurt and the sorrow and the humiliation her husband had caused her. She let it drift away because she had the best part of her marriage standing right in front of her.

"It's just temporary." *I think.* She felt tears fall.

"Aww, Mom." He came toward her. "I'm so sorry."

She didn't want to cry. She pressed her lips together

as hard as she could to keep herself from doing that, but when her son wrapped his arms around her, she couldn't contain her tears anymore. It was so silly, too. It wasn't as if they'd broken up. It was just temporary.

But was it?

She feared, oh how she feared, that they would never get back what they had. Driving away from him had solidified in her mind that she didn't just love him; she adored Bren Connelly. She loved how he treated her son. She loved his honor and his integrity. Most of all, she loved the way he loved her.

"You know what you need?" Kyle asked. "A cup of hot chocolate."

She almost started to cry all over again. It was their thing—their go-to comfort treat when the chips were down. How many times had she said that to him over the years?

"That'd be nice."

He led her to the kitchen table, encouraged her to sit down, and she was so proud of him in that moment. So full of love. At least she had Kyle. She would always have Kyle.

HE TEXTED HER, Lauren thought it would be better if she ignored the message. Who knew how far crazy Frank Farrell might go. If the man had it out for Bren, he might try and get ahold of phone records and data records. Okay, so maybe that was far-fetched, but she didn't want to take a chance. So she ignored the messages.

She couldn't ignore Bren entirely. Though it pained her to do so, she monitored the comments on the infamous photo. Eventually the comments died down, but it was obvious someone kept pushing it to the top of the feed, because just when there was no activity, boom, it'd reappear again. Whatever. She had more important things to worry about. She finally found a job. There was the stress of that, plus dealing with school. Kyle continued with his steer riding, though Jax volunteered to take him to his lessons. His next competition wasn't until mid-March, and as the day approached, she tried not to think about the fact that Bren would be there.

"You going to be okay?"

Kyle's concerned brown eyes fixed on her as they headed toward the Via Del Caballo Rodeo Grounds.

"I'll be fine," she said.

"You know everyone will be there."

As if that should concern her. As if she might be embarrassed about that picture, still. He was trying to protect her. That made her want to cry all over again.

"I know." She couldn't help but glance around as they pulled into the rodeo grounds. No big black truck. "But nothing ever came of that photo."

She slid into a spot next to a big truck and horse trailer. "Are the kids at school still teasing you?"

Her son didn't answer at first, and she supposed that was answer enough.

"Not anymore," he finally admitted.

She turned her car off, facing him, for some reason surprised by his answer. "What made them stop?"

He faced her, too, and he looked so adorable sitting in the passenger seat, his straw hat pulled down low. One day the girls would be chasing after him, but for now he maintained his boyish look of innocence.

"I knocked the stuffin' out of one of them."

"You *what*?" She almost dropped her keys.

"Shawn asked me if you were still doing that police

officer and then Wyatt said you'd probably moved on to doing firefighters and then Harley said something and I just sort of let them have it."

"With your fists?"

"Actually, that's the weird thing. I knocked Shawn over with a single blow. Turns out my riding lessons have really helped me muscle up. Bren said that's because riding is like swimming. You don't know how much work it is until you start building muscle."

"You told Bren about this?"

Kyle nodded. "I was afraid to tell you."

With good reason, but she wished Bren had let her know. "What did he say?"

"That sometimes you have to take a stand. He said that's what soldiers do all the time. They don't let anyone bully them, but first they always try to settle things peacefully. He was kind of mad that I didn't do that, but, Mom, what else could I do? I tried ignoring them and they wouldn't leave me alone."

So he'd gotten into a fistfight to protect her honor. If it wouldn't send the wrong message, she would have hugged him.

"And have they left you alone?"

He nodded, his hat casting shadows on his face. It was another beautiful day in Via Del Caballo, her son's eyes bright with something like relief.

"They haven't said a word about you since."

He was proud of that fact. Her little man had settled his own differences. "You should never hit someone."

"That's what Bren said."

"Bren's right."

He gave her a look that immediately made her grow still. "Why don't you see him anymore?"

She took a deep breath. "It's complicated."

"Uncle Jax said you crapped out on courage."

"He *what*?" Man, there was no end to the surprising things her son was telling her today.

"He said Bren did, too. He said that the both of you need to pull your heads out of your asses."

"Kyle! Don't swear."

"Sorry, Mom." He held her gaze. "I just think he's kind of right."

"You do?"

He nodded. "I didn't at first. I mean, I was kind of glad you broke up. But you're so sad, Mom. I hate seeing you like that."

Where was a box of Kleenex when you needed one? "I'm okay."

"No, Mom. You're not. You try to pretend you are, but you're not."

No. She really wasn't.

"Are you going to marry him?"

She felt the breath leave her. "No."

"Why not?"

She reminded herself to breathe again. "It's complicated."

He shook his head in disgust. "That's what adults always say, but I think it's a cop-out. You're miserable without him, Mom. He's miserable without you. I say the two of you are being stupid."

And with that, he opened the door and ran off, and it was only when she saw him catch up with another kid that she realized he'd run off to catch up with a friend.

The two of you are being stupid.

Were they?

One thing was for certain—as she left her car, she

felt a whole lot calmer all of a sudden. That was weird because usually she was a complete stress mess on rodeo days. But she had to admit, she felt almost light.

Kyle approved.

It wasn't until he'd said the words that she realized how much his disapproval had bothered her. Not that he'd ever discouraged her outwardly, but she could tell the thought of her getting involved with a man had bothered him. At first.

She inhaled a deep breath of sage-scented air. It was late afternoon, and as she headed toward the grandstands nestled into the side of a hill, she paused for a moment.

Back to where it all started: the Via Del Caballo Rodeo Grounds.

Back where she'd first met Bren. Back where Kyle had first ridden a steer. Back to where she'd watched her first rodeo.

Home.

And it was. The place had settled into her heart in a way she would have never imagined. She loved the oak trees that dotted the rodeo grounds. Loved the mountains in the distance. Loved the way everyone smiled in greeting as she walked past them. Up ahead she could see the announcer's stand. It presided over wooden chutes recently given a new coat of white paint, the color extra bright.

And there he was.

The man of her dreams. Or the man who haunted her dreams. He leaned against the white chute, one leg drawn up, his heel resting on the bottom rung of the chute. He stared at her, his black cowboy hat shielding his eyes, but she knew he watched her.

She loved him.

She'd thought maybe she'd been kidding herself. Love didn't happen so quickly. After Paul, she hadn't even been sure she believed in happily-ever-afters, but she knew what she felt for Bren was real because it nearly took her breath away.

"Hey," she said.

"Hey," was all he said back, his brown eyes staring at her so intently she wanted to bow her head.

"How you been?" Lord, could she sound any more trite?

"Good." He stood there. "You?"

Horrible. Awful. She cried herself to sleep a lot. Kyle didn't know the half of just how miserable she'd been.

"Good," she lied.

He nodded, turned away. She lifted a hand.

Marry me.

His words sounded in her ears as clearly as if he'd spoken them again, but he hadn't. She watched him walk away and she realized she'd been a coward. He'd been willing to risk it all and she'd walked away.

You had his best interest at heart.

But had she? Or had she had her own? Had she been too afraid to commit? Too afraid of repeating the mistakes of her past? Afraid of committing herself to one man because the last time she'd done that, it'd been horrible. The truth was, though, that Bren was as different from Paul as air was from water. He *was* the air she breathed.

"I drew Crossfired."

She turned and there stood Kyle, her son's eyes the most serious she'd ever seen them. He glanced at Bren and she thought he might say something to him, call

him back because it was clear Bren hadn't seen him
walk up. But he didn't. Instead he cocked his head to
the side.

"He's a good steer. Big."

She swallowed. "How big?"

"As big as a bull, Mom."

The words should have filled her with fear, but for
the first time she understood that her son's courage far
outmatched her own. He wasn't afraid of anything. Not
the father who used to bully his mom. Not the bullies
who taunted him. Not a thousand-pound animal that
might buck him off.

"You should have no problem, then." And she meant
every word. "You've been preparing to step it up. Now's
your chance."

Her son's chin tipped up, and he stared at her with
such pride that her heart swelled to triple its size. How
had she raised such an amazing little man?

"I'll be up in the grandstands." She walked forward,
had to duck low so she could kiss him beneath his cowboy hat, and for once he didn't pull away or spit out a
"Mo-om."

He let her kiss him and then he said, "Love you,
Mom."

"Love you, too, kiddo."

She gave it to God then. It was out of her hands.
Whatever her son's future, she knew she'd never stand
in the way of it. He would live his life without the fear
that had clouded her own.

She barely paid attention as she headed to the grandstands, which was probably why she didn't recognize
Natalie Reynolds and her husband, Colt. Next to them
sat his sister, Claire, and her husband, Ethan, the man

responsible for her brother's relocation to Via Del Caballo.

"Lauren," said Natalie. "Sit here."

The blonde's blue eyes were wide and friendly. Colt smiled at her. So did Claire and Ethan. She barely knew any of them, but they welcomed her with open arms.

"So what's this I hear about you and our town sheriff getting cozy?" asked Colt, his own blue eyes as merry as a Christmas morning.

A month ago she would have blushed three shades of red. A week ago she might even have denied it. Today she just sat down next to them and said, "What can I say? I have a thing for older men."

"Oh, yeah?" Colt asked. "I know a few old men who might like a date with a young thing like you."

"Colt," said his wife, elbowing him.

"That's okay." Lauren included the whole family in her own smile. "I'm off the market."

Colt's eyes widened. So did Natalie's.

"Really?" he asked.

She faced the arena, and even from a distance she could still spot Bren standing near the chutes. He was talking to someone now, a little blonde. She should have felt jealous, but she didn't. She'd seen the look in his eyes earlier. He loved her. Still. She wiggled her toes in sudden delight.

"What steer did your son draw?" Ethan asked.

The dark-haired man was more serious than his brother-in-law. But she liked Ethan McCall. He'd always been nice to her when he'd come out on a vet call to consult with her brother on DTS Ranch.

"Crossfired."

Colt winced. "That's a tough one."

"Not for my son."

"Lauren's right. Her son's a really good rider. I'll have him jumping 1.10 meters in no time."

"High praise indeed," said Colt's sister.

A drill team started lining up at the gate and Lauren knew from experience that the rodeo was about to start. Sure enough, the announcer gave a ten-minute call, but she became lost in her thoughts. She'd settled into life in Via Del Caballo to the point that she couldn't imagine living anywhere else. And as she looked around, she was suddenly grateful for all the blessings in her life. She was lucky. She'd had some hard knocks, but she'd picked herself up and brushed the dirt off. Her brother had helped carry her, and for that she would always be grateful. He'd been called out of town on business—otherwise he would have been with her today. His presence was the only thing missing right now to make her happiness complete.

When the steer riding started, for once her heart didn't try to break out of her chest. When the first rider was thrown a good twenty feet into the air, she winced, but she didn't hide her face. She knew enough by now to know that he landed okay and that he would be fine. A little humiliated at the short amount of time he'd ridden, but okay. When it came to Kyle's turn, she leaned forward a bit, but that was it. She saw Bren standing above him. There were a few other faces she recognized helping him, too. Friends who rode with him. Everyone helped everyone on the junior rodeo circuit.

"Well, now, ladies and gentlemen, how about a round of applause for a hometown kid. This is Kyle Danners riding Crossfired."

The Reynolds clan whooped so loud it nearly deafened her, but it brought a smile to her face, too. These were her friends now, their hometown crowd, their extended family.

And then the gate swung open. Her breath caught. She came halfway out of her seat because Crossfired jumped so high she didn't think there was any way Kyle could hang on. He did. Her son's legs seemed to be glued to the steer's side, and Kyle had been right. A big steer, as big as a bull. The animal swung left and then right, his back end so high off the ground Kyle could have reached between the steer's ears and touched the earth below him. Or so it seemed.

And still he rode.

That's when she started screaming. So did Colt and Natalie and Claire and Ethan. The whole place erupted and she couldn't breathe as five seconds turned into six and then seven and finally eight.

He jumped off like a seasoned pro.

"Unbelievable!" Colt cried. "Amazing."

Ethan leaned forward. "Your son's going to be a star."

She clapped her palms to her cheeks. Her hands came away wet. He'd done it. He'd ridden the biggest steer of his life...and he'd made it look easy.

"Ladies and gentlemen, there's your new leader right there," cried the announcer. "Ninety-one! Unbelievable."

"Ninety-one," said Colt. "Damn."

Even she knew that was a good score, and since Kyle wasn't performing in slack, they would know if he won in just a few minutes. Only three more riders to go.

"I'm going to head down." She got up, and she was surprised to note her legs were weak. Maybe she wasn't as calm, cool and collected as she'd thought.

"Tell him congratulations," said Natalie.

"I'm going to tell people I knew him when," Ethan said.

"I know," said Claire. "It's too bad Jax had to miss this."

"I'm sure someone caught it on video," said Colt.

Her footfalls were light as she headed toward the chutes. She heard the crowd cheer only to immediately groan, and she knew without looking that the next rider had fallen short. Same deal with the next one. Only one more rider to go, and so she paused near the side of the arena, leaning down so she could peer through the slats at the last competitor.

He fell off after two jumps.

She rested her head on the board, the wood cool to the touch, grateful for the support. He'd done it. Her baby boy had won his first buckle. The first of many, she knew. Bren had been right all those weeks ago. Kyle had what it took to be not just good at what he loved but great.

"He did it."

She jerked upright. She hadn't even heard him approach. But then, how would she over the din of the crowd.

She turned, slowly, having to take a deep breath before she looked into his eyes. "He did it." She took a step toward him. "Thanks to you."

He shook his head. "Don't look at me. Kyle put in all the hard work."

"Yes, but he knew what to focus on thanks to you."

His caramel-colored eyes darkened. She saw his gaze fix on her lips and she felt herself lean forward.

"Bren, I can't—"

"Lauren, I don't—"

They both stopped talking, and for reasons she couldn't explain, Lauren suddenly wanted to laugh. She wasn't nervous anymore. She didn't feel restless. She didn't feel anything other than pure, unabashed love... love that she hoped he spotted.

"Mom! Did you see? Did you see?"

Kyle came running up to her, the biggest grin that she'd ever seen on his face. She instantly opened her arms. He rushed into them, hugging her tight, bringing her to tears for about the tenth time that day.

He might be a steer rider, but he was still her little boy.

"Did you see it or did you hide your face again?"

She laughed. She couldn't help it. "Are you kidding? I couldn't look away." She clutched his shoulders, shaking him a little. "That was the best. The absolute *best* ride I've ever seen."

Her son's face was the sunshine on a summer morning. The glow of a millions stars. A whole ocean of happiness.

"I think I might have won."

"Think?" Bren said. "I know you did."

"Well, I don't know what the other kids scored—"

"Yup," said the announcer. "It's official. Kyle Danners is your steer-riding champion."

Her son, the little boy who tried so hard to seem grown up, let out a whoop of delight reminiscent of when he was five.

"I did it." He jumped up and down. "I did it." And then he jumped up and down some more.

"Yep," she said. "You did."

He all but ran back toward the chutes.

"He should cut through the arena. It'll be shorter."

"I don't think he cares."

They both turned to follow, but before she took a step, Bren stopped her with an outstretched hand. She knew what he was asking then, knew that if she took it, they were calling a truce to their forced exile. That from here on out, they would be together, through thick and thin. That whatever the future brought, they would face it together.

Her hand slipped into his.

They walked hand in hand into the arena, the two of them standing side by side as Kyle accepted his first buckle. And when it came time for him to say a few words, she couldn't keep tears from falling as he thanked Bren and his uncle, but most of all her.

She glanced up at Bren. There were tears in his eyes, too. And then he was kissing her. She kissed him back, right there in front of God and half the town of Via Del Caballo and she didn't care. Neither of them cared because they had each other.

"Mo-om," she heard Kyle cry.

And then they drew back, and they were laughing, and when Kyle came over, they hugged him, and then Bren pulled her up against his side and she knew that this was where she wanted to be for the rest of her life.

Epilogue

It was controlled chaos in the campaign office of one Sheriff Bren Connelly. The final moments had kicked down and at any second a winner would be declared.

"Well, if we don't pull this off, it won't be for lack of trying," said Jerry, the man sweating even though it was a cool June evening.

"If we don't pull this off, I'm never hiring you again," Bren said, resplendent in his black sheriff's uniform. Around him were a number of his deputies, and even though it really shouldn't surprise her, Lauren was touched by the support. They had no way of knowing if Bren would win. Everyone had known it would be a tight race, and it had been. Right now the polls showed Bren leading by a narrow 5 percent margin, but that could change.

She glanced at the clock.

"Relax, honey, I've got this."

She glanced up at the man she loved and knew he did have this. Whatever the outcome was, they would be okay.

"I just wish it were over already," she admitted.

"It will be soon," said her brother, coming up to stand alongside her. He'd recently returned from yet another one of his business trips. The last one for a while, he'd promised. She hoped so, because she'd set up a surprise. She'd be moving out of the apartment soon and in with Bren. She didn't want Jax rambling around in his big old home all by himself, so she'd suggested he hire a housekeeper/cook, a woman named Naomi Jones who came highly recommended. He would grumble when she told him about the interview she'd set up, but he had no choice. She wanted her brother to be happy, and it just so happened that Naomi was gorgeous. Bren said she was trying to matchmake. Kyle wasn't so couth. He'd called her a pimp. She'd threatened to wash his mouth out with soap.

A hand slipped into her own.

"Whatever happens," he said for her ears only.

"Whatever happens."

It'd become their slogan in recent weeks. She looked up and smiled. He clutched her hand so hard the brand-new two-carat diamond ring that still felt strange on her finger must have left a dent in his own palm. She knew then that he wasn't as blasé as he might seem.

Whatever happened.

They'd done everything they could to help him win. Jerry had been a miracle worker. When they'd announced to the world that they were a couple, Jerry had immediately gone to work. He'd enlisted the aid of a PR strategist, a woman named Emily who'd worked her butt off to take care of damage control. As it turned out, there was no damage. The citizens of Via Del Caballo were a lot more laid-back about their age difference than they'd given them credit for. Sure, there'd been a few snickers here and there, but nobody had really cared and Emily had made sure that the citizens of Via Del

Caballo all knew that she was about to graduate in the fall with a bachelor of science in nursing.

"Here it is!"

It was Kyle who'd called the words, her son peering intently up at the television screen in the one-room office that used to be a deli.

"And in a tight race for the seat of Via Del Caballo sheriff, incumbent Bren Connelly earned 62 percent of the votes, narrowly beating out challenger Hank Cresta."

People screamed. Bren was immediately clapped on the back by one of his deputies. Someone pulled her into their arms. Natalie, she realized. The whole Reynolds clan had shown up and offered support. Lauren thought it seemed like a dream.

He'd won.

He'd really won.

Someone started chanting, "Four more years. Four more years." Soon the whole room was shouting the words. Bren pulled her into his arms.

"Well," he asked, "what do you say? You want to do this again in four years?"

She slipped her hands around his waist, holding him tight. "I'm willing to do it for as long as you like."

His eyes glinted and she knew his mind had gone down a road she hadn't intended. She laughed. He did, too, and then he was kissing her and the crowd went crazy for a whole other reason when Kyle cried out, "Mo-om!"

* * * * *

REQUEST YOUR FREE BOOKS!
2 FREE NOVELS PLUS 2 FREE GIFTS!

✦ HARLEQUIN®

⌐Western ℛomance

ROMANCE THE ALL-AMERICAN WAY!

YES! Please send me 2 FREE Harlequin® Western Romance novels and my 2 FREE gifts (gifts are worth about $10). After receiving them, if I don't wish to receive any more books, I can return the shipping statement marked "cancel." If I don't cancel, I will receive 4 brand-new novels every month and be billed just $4.74 per book in the U.S. or $5.49 per book in Canada. That's a savings of at least 12% off the cover price! It's quite a bargain! Shipping and handling is just 50¢ per book in the U.S. and 75¢ per book in Canada.* I understand that accepting the 2 free books and gifts places me under no obligation to buy anything. I can always return a shipment and cancel at any time. Even if I never buy another book, the two free books and gifts are mine to keep forever.

154/354 HDN GJ5V

Name	
	(PLEASE PRINT)

Address	Apt. #

City	State/Prov.	Zip/Postal Code

Signature (if under 18, a parent or guardian must sign)

Mail to the **Reader Service:**
IN U.S.A.: P.O. Box 1867, Buffalo, NY 14240-1867
IN CANADA: P.O. Box 609, Fort Erie, Ontario L2A 5X3

Want to try two free books from another line?
Call 1-800-873-8635 or visit www.ReaderService.com.

* Terms and prices subject to change without notice. Prices do not include applicable taxes. Sales tax applicable in N.Y. Canadian residents will be charged applicable taxes. Offer not valid in Quebec. This offer is limited to one order per household. Not valid for current subscribers to Harlequin Western Romance books. All orders subject to credit approval. Credit or debit balances in a customer's account(s) may be offset by any other outstanding balance owed by or to the customer. Please allow 4 to 6 weeks for delivery. Offer available while quantities last.

Your Privacy—The Reader Service is committed to protecting your privacy. Our Privacy Policy is available online at www.ReaderService.com or upon request from the Reader Service.

We make a portion of our mailing list available to reputable third parties that offer products we believe may interest you. If you prefer that we not exchange your name with third parties, or if you wish to clarify or modify your communication preferences, please visit us at www.ReaderService.com/consumerschoice or write to us at Reader Service Preference Service, P.O. Box 9062, Buffalo, NY 14240-9062. Include your complete name and address.

HWR16

"Miss Caraway, I'd like you to work with Fester."

"I have no experience with horses, Dr. Boone."

"Archer." He sat in the chair opposite her. "I know you've never worked with animals before. But you're smart. Your eyes…" He cleared his throat before trying again. "You're smart. Fester seems to respond favorably to you, and I can show you a few things that might help."

What about her eyes? "You can't work with Fester yourself?"

"He barely tolerates me. I'd like you to help him."

She drew in an unsteady breath. "I can't. Thank you."

"Can't isn't a philosophy I subscribe to, Miss Caraway."

She bit back a smile. She appreciated his determination. But he wouldn't feel the same when she was a Monroe again. "Dr. Boone, I'm afraid things might get a bit more complicated."

He frowned. "Why?"

Because I'm lying to you about who I am. "My children are arriving today."

"Children?" His surprise was obvious.

She nodded. "I have two."

He opened his mouth, closed it, then said, "Surely your husband—"

"My personal life is my own, Dr. Boone." She straightened in her chair. "I informed you only so you'd understand my answer to your offer."

He continued frowning at her.

He could frown all he wanted but she wasn't here to help him. She was here for her father.

"I apologize for prying." Archer's expression had faded into something softer, something vulnerable and searching.

"No apologies necessary."

Eden stared—she couldn't help it. He wanted to help Fester, wanted the *animal* to be happy. Yes, he was a little rough around the edges, but he was direct—not rude necessarily. And he was incredibly handsome. So far everything she'd learned about Dr. Boone was good. It would be easier if he'd been misspending grant funds or his work ethic was suspect or his facility was dangerous or out of compliance. None of which was the case. Worse, she found herself respecting his single-minded, detail-oriented, fiery loyalty to his work.

If he ever used that undivided focus on a woman…

Don't miss A COWBOY TO CALL DADDY
by Sasha Summers, available March 2017 wherever
Harlequin® Western Romance
books and ebooks are sold.

www.Harlequin.com

HWREXP0217